The Soldier & The Actress

INSPIRING ROMANCE SUSPENSE

COLEVILLE RANCH ROMANCES
BOOK THREE

CAMI CHECKETTS

Birch River
PUBLISHING

The Soldier & The Actress: Coleville Ranch Romances #3

Copyright © 2024 by Cami Checketts

All rights reserved.

No part of this book may be reproduced in any form or by any electronic or mechanical means, including information storage and retrieval systems, without written permission from the author, except for the use of brief quotations in a book review.

Editing: Daniel Coleman and Ceara Nobles

Cover Art: Novak Illustrations

Free Book

Sign up for my newsletter and receive exclusive deals, giveaways, and your free copy of *Her Best Friend Romance Collection* (4 Complete Romance Novels) on BookFunnel.

Character List

Lieutenant Miles Coleville - Navy SEAL. Close friend of Quaid Raven and Aiden Porter. Humble, tough, loyal.

Eva Chevron - A-list actress from a Wyoming ranch. Fun, bright, happy, and in danger.

Sheriff Clint Coleville - tough, closed off, protective, big brother of the Coleville family. Find Clint and Lily Lillywhite's story in *The Sheriff & the Nurse.*

Easton Coleville - bull rider, twin brother of Walker, younger brother of Miles, charming, hilarious, outspoken.

Walker Coleville - roper, twin brother of Easton, younger brother of Miles, thoughtful and kind. Find Walker's story in *The Roper & The Author.*

Captain Aiden Porter - Charming, talented, handsome, second-top security specialist in the world. Find Aiden and Chalisa's story in *Impossible Crusade, A Chance for Charity Romance #5*.

Air Force Reconnaissance Lieutenant Paul Braven - Aiden Porter's pilot and security specialist. Find Paul's story in *The Pilot & The Athlete*.

Autumn Cardon - Female warrior, employed by Aiden Porter, hilarious, flirtatious.
    Find Autumn and Jarom Love's story in *The Female Warrior and The Charming Gentleman*, Coleville Ranch Romances #7.

Lieutenant Hays West - Tough, kind, loyal. Navy SEAL. Has been in love with Elizabeth Oliver for years.
    Elizabeth Oliver - Oldest sister of Thomas (Quaid Raven) and Jacey Oliver. Find Hays and Elizabeth's story in *The Bodyguard & The Billionaire*.

Lieutenant Cade Miller - Retired Army hero, recipient of the Silver Star, heartbroken, recluse, cowboy.
    Jacqueline (Jacey) Oliver - Youngest daughter of the beaten-down Benjamin and manipulative and murderous Catherine Oliver. Find Cade and Jacey's story in *The Recluse & The Fugitive*.

Thomas Oliver (Lieutenant Quaid Raven) - Elizabeth's younger brother, married to Anna Marley. Find their story in *Impossible Climb, A Chance for Charity Romance #4*.

Captain Jagger and Belinda (Bee) Lemuel - Hays's best friends. Find their story in *Impossible Chase*.

Sutton Smith - Top security specialist in the world currently. Aiden's surrogate father and idol. Find Sutton and Duchess Elizabeth Gunthry (Liz) story in *The Captivating Warrior*.

Did I forget anyone? I apologize if I did! I always try to introduce each character when they appear in a book so don't feel like you need to memorize this character list.

If you have any questions, please email me cami@camichecketts.com. With over 170 books out, it's sometimes hard for me to keep track of the characters! The character info is repeated at the end of the novel if you want to simply read and enjoy and find other characters' stories after.

Hugs and thanks,
Cami

Coleville Ranch Romance

The Recluse & The Fugitive – Cade Miller and Jacqueline Oliver

The Bodyguard & The Billionaire – Lieutenant Hays West and Elizabeth Oliver

The Soldier & The Actress - Lieutenant Miles Coleville and Eva Chevron

The Pilot & The Athlete – Lieutenant Paul Braven and Shay Cannon

The Sheriff & the Nurse – Clint Coleville and Lily Lillywhite

The Roper & The Author – Walker Coleville and Marci Richards

The Female Warrior and The Charming Gentleman – Jarom Love and Autumn Cardon

CHAPTER
One

EVA CHEVRON PERCHED ON TIPTOES, arms up to the sky as she attempted to meditate on the back patio of her Balboa Peninsula home, watching the sun set over the Pacific Ocean and counting her blessings. A loving family, good health, faith in heaven above, success in her dream job, a beautiful August evening, and another day that Jorge Augilar was in prison.

The renowned drug dealer had been captured by the famed Aiden Porter six months ago. Aiden had kept his involvement under the radar from the media, but Eva's assigned FBI agent, Ryken Anderson, had name-dropped. People in Hollywood loved to do that, but Aiden Porter was a big name to drop. He was the second top security specialist in the world next to the legendary Sutton Smith.

The problem was, Jorge had recently become obsessed with Eva. At least that was how Agent Henderson, 'Ryken to only you Eva' with a subtle wink, described the 'issue.' Obsessed wasn't strong enough in Eva's mind. Not for the nonstop messages Jorge sent through multiple channels—emails, typed notes, social media messages. Obsessed? How about fanatical? Zealous? Maniacal? One of those might fit better.

Ryken assured her the prison guards had taken away Jorge's privileges to communicate with the outside world, but the notes hadn't stopped. He had too many connections and, honestly, what were some love notes to a famous actress compared to his long list of horrific crimes?

Eva pushed out a heavy breath and glanced at her Fitbit to see how long she'd been meditating, or rather 'gnawing like a dog on his bone' as her dad would say while she stressed about Jorge.

Fifty seconds? Ah, heck no. The wellness coach her agent 'recommended' said if she could meditate for five minutes, it would help reduce the stress of a murderous drug lord sending messages that he was 'coming for his favorite actress.'

She knew the coach meant well, but he didn't have the foul, murderous, despicable Jorge Augilar after him, now did he?

Eva had dealt with stalkers before. Why did this one bother her so much?

Meditation. Clear thoughts. Focus. She'd found if she meditated outside, focused on the view instead of closing her eyes, held difficult poses instead of lying down, and fixated on her gratitude list to the good Lord above, she could sometimes make it to the elusive five minutes.

Who was she lying to? She'd never made it past eighty seconds. Patience and standing still had never been her strong suits, though she could pretend both when acting. Her mom had constantly begged her to stop dancing around the house and breaking things. Her dad had teased her whenever she claimed she was 'being calm' through gritted teeth. He'd chuckle and say, 'You know, darlin', you can lie to some of the people some of the time ...'

Eva smiled. She missed her parents, sisters, friends, and extended family near Cody, Wyoming. Hollywood interactions were a far stretch from the 'good-old boys' and 'down-home gals' she'd grown up with. She loved her career and thrived on playing a variety of roles to exactness, but she didn't appreciate the shallow relationships, underhanded deals, and backstabbing.

She'd learned the hard way over the past ten years not to trust easily, and to steer clear of romantic relationships. Every celebrity she'd dated when she first arrived was looking for the next big thing and dumped her as soon as a better option came along. She thought she'd learned her lesson and went years maintaining an emotional distance. Then she fell for Lake Eastwood a year ago. He'd made Eva feel like she was his entire world, then cheated on her with both Bermuda Venus and Jezebel Noir. That one had hurt. Though she should've expected it, he was a fantastic actor. Why had she been so surprised he'd only been acting with her?

Please help me not to fall for a famous, unfaithful man again. Please show me the light. Shine a beam on the man I can trust. A man who can be loyal and not dump me for the next hot option.

Looking out over the peaceful beach, the sun lighting the clouds red, orange, and pink as it touched the ocean, she noticed a lone man approaching at a quick jog. The setting sun highlighted his strong form like a halo. She sucked in a breath. Was it just a random coincidence or was heaven above giving her a sign?

She leaned into the balcony wall, anxious to see the man clearly. She knew she should be wary. Her house alarms and cameras were on, but maybe she should hire a security team. She rolled her eyes. Jorge wasn't going to send some jogger to attack her. All California beaches were public and a man running wasn't an anomaly. The stretch of beach behind her house was quiet without a public access close. She saw joggers in the morning and sometimes walkers in the evening, but most people didn't want to haul their beach gear too far from a public parking area.

The man got closer, and her heart beat quicker. She wasn't certain if it was anticipation or anxiety. This could be her dream man or a hit man.

She could now distinguish dark hair and a tall, well-built body. He was still too far away to distinguish facial features, but he was moving fast. If he angled away from the water and toward the houses, he'd reach her within seconds. Then he would be one Superman leap from the sand to her patio. She could be dead or kidnapped before she could squeak for help.

Thank you for that image, she snapped at her morbid mind. She needed to be cautious but not a Nervous Nellie. She knew it was in her best interest that she'd morphed from an 'innocent Wyoming cowgirl' to 'famous but still humble' to petrified and disturbed in the course of ten short years. No news media had pinned the last two terms on her. She'd hid the pain over Lake's betrayal and the fear of Jorge's relentless pursuit from them pretty well, if she did say so herself.

She pulled her cell phone out of her pocket and clicked on the phone app, just in case the man was coming for her. Sun halo aside, she doubted heaven was sending her dream man running down the beach.

Ryken had asked her to call him instead of 911. He promised he would get the right people moving faster if she was in danger. Despite his obnoxious flirtations, she appreciated his diligence in protecting her.

Lake had begged her to call him first when he'd somehow found out she was in dire straits and dropped by to visit last week. Yeah, right; she'd call him as fast as she'd pick up a rattlesnake. She'd told him to drop dead in a ditch. He'd appreciated that. She could still see his fake green eyes snapping at her from his too-tight, too-tanned face as he told her, 'Don't think your Idaho redneck lingo is going to win you any roles without me. You'll be crawling back in no time.'

Idaho? Come on. He didn't know the first thing about the real Eva Chevron. Not that it mattered to Lake and not that there was anything wrong with Idaho, but she was proud to be from Wyoming.

She hadn't even considered crawling back to him. He'd cheated on her, twice, and then spent the past six months alternating between trying to woo her back or threatening her with losing roles or popularity when she didn't take his bait. She'd done brilliantly with her career, rising higher without him. Scum ball anyway.

The fit runner man kept racing along the beach, but he wasn't angling in her direction. She should go back inside, but she found herself fascinated that the dying sun was still highlighting him. The halo she'd prayed for, maybe? No, that was far-reaching, and despite her love for acting and drama, Eva was as practical as they came. She had to be to survive emotionally in the Hollywood rat race.

Maybe she was simply fascinated that such a large man could run at his speed. The smooth lines of muscle working in synchrony in his arms and legs were enthralling. How did the song go? *Six foot four and full of muscle*? She'd guess those stats were correct.

His profile was clear to her now as he was almost parallel to her patio and the sun had descended, leaving it light enough to see him without the 'halo' interference.

There was no denying he was a strikingly handsome man. The sculpted lines of a 'manly macho male man' as her sister Tasha would say.

She barked out a laugh, thinking of Tasha saying that redundant phrase in a goofy voice and how silly Eva was being ogling some guy she didn't know and would never know.

At her too-loud laugh, the running man glanced her direction. The breath whooshed out of her as she stared into startling blue eyes framed by dark lashes and brows. The patio shifted beneath her, and she had to cling to the railing to stay on her feet. It was like heaven had slapped her in the face.

He was definitely handsome. Exquisite. Ideal. Swoony. But the impact of him looking at her felt much deeper than any other beautiful man looking her way. She'd met thousands of handsome men the past ten years. Something about this man felt significant.

His lips curved up in a slow, enticing smile. He slowed to a walk and then paused and raised a hand to her. An arc of connection surged through the air between them. It washed over her like an enchanted breeze. Leaps beyond what Hollywood could try to create. Who was this man, and why did she feel like she'd just locked eyes with her future?

She froze, stunned by the unfamiliar feelings his eyes focused on her had created. Could this be an answer to her prayer? It all felt unrealistic, almost surreal, and somehow the most genuine and authentic connection she'd ever experienced.

She had no idea how to respond. She didn't wave. She didn't call out to him. She didn't do a dang thing but smile and stare.

He waited another beat and then the hope in his eyes waned. He tilted his chin up to her and raced off, heading south to the point.

Oh, no. Her soul cried out for him to stop, turn around, come back.

No. That was silly. It was a good thing. Definitely a good thing. Her rational, safe mind knew it was a good thing. Agent Henderson and her dad would agree. She shouldn't be talking to or encouraging strangers.

Her heart that was palpitating, her hands that were trembling, and her mind that was swooning over one look from that man's blue eyes thought it was an awful thing. Why had she been unable to respond and let him run off? Why hadn't she called him back or chased after him?

She couldn't lie to herself and anticipate seeing him again. She'd lived here for three years and had never seen him running on the beach.

He ran off even faster than he'd approached. A fine picture for sure. She almost snapped a photo with her phone but restrained. Being the object of far too many unapproved-by-her photos, she'd never take one of someone else. Even if the blue-eyed hunk's enticing form in a T-shirt and shorts was something she never wanted to forget.

Darkness crept over the beach. Still, she didn't move. Her fantasy man was long gone. Would he come back this direction if she waited long enough?

Wow. If anybody knew *the* Eva Chevron was having desperate thoughts about a man she didn't know because she'd said a prayer, felt a connection, and been captured by his blue eyes … it would make headlines.

She smiled, shook her head, turned, and smacked into a wall of hard flesh in black clothing.

"Help!" she cried out before the man flipped her to face away from him, clapped a hand over her mouth, and pinned her against him with a thick arm like a steel clamp around her chest.

Eva's arms were trapped, her cell phone still in her hand. She writhed to free herself, clinging to the side buttons that were supposed to call 911 if you held them long enough.

"Drop the phone," the man snarled.

She kicked her heel back at his shin instead and dug the fingernails of her left hand into his thigh.

He cursed and smacked her hand into the half-wall surrounding the patio. She clung to the phone, but he rammed her hand against the wood again and again. Pain radiated from her hand up her arm and the phone was flung from her grasp, clattering onto the cement.

She screamed, but only a squeak escaped his tight grip. Yanking her head back to headbutt him, she caught his chin. He cursed. Her head hurt now too, but his grip loosened slightly.

Eva dropped to a heap at his feet and scrabbled away. He leaped on top of her, flattening her to the concrete between the patio couch and the decorative wooden half-wall.

"Help!" she screamed as loud as she could. She had neighbors. Would they hear her? Were they even home? Her tough, blue-eyed soulmate was unfortunately long gone. Nobody would see her down here; they'd have to hear her. "Help! Help!"

"Shut up," the man growled in her ear, grabbing a pillow off the nearby outdoor couch and shoving it over her face to muffle her screams. She couldn't breathe with the pillow covering her nose and mouth and his body weight pressing her into the unforgiving concrete.

She flailed and fought, but the lack of oxygen brought darkness to the edges of her vision and slowed her movements.

"That's better," the man said. "Ryken will give me a huge bonus for this one."

Ryken? Her mind was getting cloudy, but ... Ryken? It could not be possible that her FBI agent had sent a man to kill her. Ryken was the one protecting her from Jorge.

Please, Heavenly Father, she begged. *A little help. Bring my fantasy running man back.*

Then darkness gripped her.

CHAPTER Two

NAVY SEAL LIEUTENANT MILES COLEVILLE raced along the picturesque Newport coastline and out onto the Balboa Peninsula. He had a five-day long weekend break from Camp Pendleton and his new friend retired-Captain Aiden Porter had offered his Newport Beach mansion. The huge home was a west coast headquarters for Aiden's security teams, but nobody was using it currently.

The top-of-the-line and spacious beach retreat sure beat his one-bedroom condo just off base in Oceanside. Miles didn't need much and was rarely home, but it was nice to relax in a twenty-million-dollar mansion once in a while.

He'd need to turn around soon, or he'd run the two miles back in the dark. The dark didn't bother him; sitting alone trying to entertain himself did. Even in a gorgeous home and beach location with a food service delivering gourmet meals, he couldn't relax. He didn't like being alone. Miles soaked up the brotherhood and camaraderie of his SEAL team. He was also missing his brothers, parents, and their Montana ranch more and more.

He should be missing his sort-of-girlfriend Lily Lillywhite. Lily was great—adventurous, happy, easy-going. If his mom and hers had their way, they'd already be married. They'd grown apart over the twelve years he'd been gone from Coleville, but every time he suggested she date other people, she turned the question around and asked if he wanted to date someone else. The answer was always no. He was too busy with the SEALs to spend time dating, and he wasn't into shallow hookups.

He wouldn't have been surprised or sad if Lily decided to move on. He didn't mind having a 'girl back home' and he was loyal to her, but she should be ready to find a local man who could get married and settle down. At the same time, maybe working in a small county hospital and living in the tiny town of Coleville didn't lend itself to many dating options.

The last time he visited home six months ago for his brother Clint's failed wedding, he had taken Lily on a date. It hadn't gone well. The silences had been awkward and long as they both scrambled for something to start a real conversation, grasping at straws to reconnect after over a year of not seeing each other in person.

At the end of the night, he'd tried not to 'trip around the issue' like his brothers Walker and Easton accused him of regarding Lily. They claimed him asking her if she wanted to date other people wasn't strong enough. He needed to be firm like he would with his military career or really anything else in his life.

So Miles had told Lily they were going different directions

and needed to be done with the relationship. She needed to be free to date and find what she was looking for. Lily had broken down and sobbed. He caught words like 'missed opportunity, keeping her safe, and a wasted life'. He'd held her as tears slipped down her smooth cheeks and nothing she said made sense. He'd felt awful, rescinded his words, and apologized. When she calmed down, they'd gone home without resolving anything.

He'd regretted not breaking up with her ever since and they hadn't communicated much. He had tender feelings for Lily and hated hurting her, but they weren't right together. Stringing each other along would only hurt both of them more in the long run. She should be free to date and have a life beyond her nursing career and nurturing all the children who stayed on her parents' ranch. She was a golden girl and would find someone great.

As soon as he went home again, he'd end it for good. Unfortunately, he couldn't do it over the phone or on a video chat. That wasn't a gentleman's way, and Lily deserved better.

A laugh barked out from a house's patio to his left, interrupting his stewing.

He glanced over and his pulse sped up as he met the most intriguing pair of dark-brown eyes he had ever glimpsed. The woman smiled at him, and he slowed his pace to a walk.

The depth and sparkle in her deep-brown eyes drew him in like a fish on a line. He instantly knew ... This was his other half, the lady he should've been searching for all his life.

He smiled, paused and raised a hand, prepared to say hello, drop a charming line, ask her to please share her number so he could call her as soon as he settled his obligation to Lily. How did he explain that he couldn't ask her out immediately without looking like a darn fool?

Before he could say or do anything, it slammed into him exactly who those gorgeous eyes belonged to.

Eva Chevron. One of the top actresses in Hollywood currently and named one of the most beautiful women in the world.

He should know. His twin brothers Easton and Walker sent him pictures of her far too often—her volunteering at a children's hospital, stopping to walk with an elderly man across the street, cheering at an L.A. Kings game and wearing a number ninety-nine Wayne Gretzky jersey, Miles's favorite player of all time. His brothers loved to tease him that the famous and talented beauty, originally from a ranch and the neighboring state of Wyoming was his future wife and that he could find her since he lived in sunny California and propose as soon as he officially cut things off with Lily.

It was a hilarious tease, in all their minds, and none of them had ever said that in Lily's presence. Miles was a SEAL, always training or away on an assignment, not part of the Hollywood social scene and attending parties where he could meet the famous actress. He and his family had helped protect his close friend Quaid Raven's famous sisters, Jacqueline and Elizabeth Oliver, but that was very different from meeting *the* Eva Chevron.

Yet here Eva was ... less than forty feet away from him. He could swear a connection surged through the air and their future lit the evening sky.

He would introduce himself, channel some of his brother Easton's charm, tell her he was the man she'd been waiting for.

His stomach flipped over. Eva Chevron didn't need some rando stopping and proclaiming he was her future. She'd think he was insane, and for good reason. He also wasn't the type to profusely proclaim anything.

She didn't say anything, lift a hand, or move toward him. He could take a hint. She was ultra-famous, and he could only imagine how many men pursued her.

Tilting his chin to her, he took off. Every step away from her was painful, as if he were giving up on their future. What was he doing? Instead of slowing down, he ran faster.

He should've spoken to her. Why hadn't he taken a chance? She might've shut him down immediately, but he'd dealt with pain and failure. It wasn't the fear of rejection. If Eva would've called to him or even raised a hand, he might have taken a shot. Her smile and the intensity of her brown gaze had lit up his world, made him believe they had a unique connection.

He was fooling himself. Connection, sparks, soul mate? That was over the top and not like him at all. His brothers at arms and brothers at home would be on the ground laughing if they could hear his thoughts.

It was only because Eva was famous, his celebrity crush. So she'd smiled at him. It was well-known how kind Eva was. He'd heard her called a breath of fresh country air and unable to squash a spider, with a video of her relocating the spider off set as her fellow actors and actresses squealed and ran the other direction. Eva Chevron would've smiled a greeting at Quaid's father, the evil Benjamin Oliver.

Besides, he wasn't a free man. Miles wished more than ever that he had 'manned up' in Easton's words and officially broken up with Lily six months ago. Then he could've done something about this instant bond he felt with Eva.

He was deluding himself. Even if he had no obligations, he didn't have a chance with Eva Chevron. He only thought he knew her. How unfair was it to her that men the world over watched her movies, followed her on social media, clipped photos of her from magazine articles and deluded themselves into believing they 'knew' her, that they were meant to be with her.

Luckily, he hadn't stooped to the photo clipping obsession stage of celebrity crushes. His brothers weren't below it though and had redecorated his cabin at home with her pictures when he'd visited six months ago. He smiled. Those two were pranksters. Lily hadn't been happy about the photos. Walker had quietly taken them down when Easton was at a bull-riding event. He suspected Walker had a crush on Lily. Miles needed to break up with his long-time girlfriend, set her free, and see if his little brother caught her. The idea sounded ... freeing.

Reaching the end of the peninsula, he realized he could keep going, or he could turn around and see if Eva was still on the patio. Would it be annoying to just say 'Hey, how are ya?' and see if she responded?

He raced back down the beach, his legs churning up the distance to the out-of-anybody's-league Eva Chevron, when he heard a female scream for help.

His senses prickled and his race became a sprint. He strained to hear the call again. It had come from close to where he'd seen Eva. Was she in danger? He approached her patio and couldn't see her or anyone standing there. Was the call for help one of her neighbors? Should he call 911 or get closer to investigate?

"Help! Help! Help!" He heard the pleas from exactly where he'd seen Eva. She must be on the floor of the patio. The thick wooden enclosure made it impossible to see what was happening or who was calling for help, but he was certain it was her.

He detoured toward her lit patio. As he approached, he could see over the barrier. A large man lay on top of a much smaller body, a pillow shoved over her face, the long, dark hair splayed out on the gray concrete.

Miles didn't stop to think or question as he leaped over the railing and drilled his shoulder straight into the man's chest with the force of a wrecking ball.

The man was launched off of Eva and slammed into the couch behind him. He recovered quickly, cursed, and came back swinging.

Miles loved a good fight as much as anyone, but he had to make sure Eva was alive, not waste time brawling. He grabbed the offered fist and flipped the guy onto the concrete in a good imitation of a Judo throw. Giving his opponent no chance to react or recover, Miles landed a fist to the man's temple and followed it up with another fist, then an elbow. The huge attacker went limp and didn't respond.

Turning to Eva, he scurried to her side. She was splayed on her back, not moving. He threw the pillow to the side, felt for a pulse, and was rewarded with a strong beat.

"Thank you," he breathed to heaven above.

He bent low to check for breathing. Her warm breath on his cheek reassured him. Unconscious but breathing, and she had a strong pulse.

Before he could pull back, her eyes blinked open.

Those deep-brown eyes. They reached into his very soul, healed, strengthened, and lifted him.

Crush? No way. This was a full-blown connection at first glance and love at second glance. He smiled. If any of his brothers could hear his thoughts, he'd never live it down. But they weren't staring into Eva Chevron's long-lashed, chocolate-brown, soul-capturing eyes.

"What ... You ..." She blinked at him as if she felt then draw but then fear filled her gaze and she squeaked out, "Please. Can you help me?"

"It's okay." He eased back onto his haunches and pointed at the unconscious man. "He's out cold. We'll get the police on their way."

She looked from the man to him and back. "Thank you," she whispered, closing her eyes as if her head were exploding. It probably was. Waking up after being knocked unconscious wasn't a great feeling. He'd been there.

Eva sat up, holding her head and staring at him. "Who are you?"

"I'm Miles."

"The runner," she said, recognition filling her eyes.

"Yes, ma'am. I turned around to head back and heard you yell for help."

"Thank you again. You saved my life." Her voice was breathless. Did that have anything to do with him and the intense draw he imagined they had between them or almost being killed?

"It's nothing." He smiled at her, and she tentatively returned it. Saving her life wasn't nothing, but he'd never be the guy to brag about being her hero. Even if he wanted to be.

The man groaned and stirred. Miles coolly pivoted toward him, rolled him onto his stomach, and pinned him down, yanking his arm behind his back. The man cursed and flailed. By simply sliding the man's wrist a couple inches higher toward his neck, Miles got him into a state of tense, though unmoving, compliance.

"You wouldn't happen to have some rope?" Miles asked.

"Of course I do." She sprang to her feet but swayed.

"Take it slow," Miles cautioned. "He's not going anywhere."

She grinned at him. Grinned. Miles almost lost his grip on the improbable yoga stretch the perp was maintaining. "You are some kind of superhero, aren't you, military man?"

Miles couldn't resist grinning back, ignoring the curses and threats the perp was uttering. How did she know he was military? "No, ma'am. Just a cowboy doing a good turn."

"A cowboy and a soldier?" She whistled and looked him over. "Now that is quite the appealing combination."

Was Eva Chevron flirting with him? His chest expanded and his cheeks heated up. Miles had never been so tempted to share that he was a Navy SEAL Lieutenant. His papa had taught them not to brag or puff themselves up, even though Mama bragged about her sons to anyone who would listen. He held his tongue.

"Thank you."

The man bucked underneath him. Miles applied more pressure with his knee and yanked the wrist hard, millimeters away from breaking it. The man yelped and cursed more foul than ever in response. "This isn't worth it. Ryken can go to—"

Miles put his free hand on the man's head and leaned on it, instantly silencing him. "There now. No need to go cussing around the lady."

Eva barked out a laugh, then held her head with a groan. He loved her barking laugh. It was as genuine as she was. He'd heard that laugh on a couple of interviews and one of the movies she'd been in.

"The rope," she said. "I shall return, brave soldier."

Miles laughed at that, more drawn to her than ever. She was the brave one. There were scratches on her arms and a future bruise on her face and she was complimenting him and running to get a rope like she was one of his men, working together like teammates, not a famous actress.

She hurried through the patio and into the rear door of the house.

Miles was left alone with the brute. He released the man's head. "Can you control that flapping jaw or do you want me to break your arm?"

"I'll be good," he croaked.

"Good. Now, who is Ryken?" he asked. The police could query the man, but Miles would love to get some inside information that could help the innocent and beautiful actress stay safe. Maybe she would need Aiden Porter's assistance. Miles could take her back to the house, get to know her, help out for the next four days until he had to get back to base on Tuesday.

"Nobody," the man spit back.

"All right. The arm broken then?" Miles increased the pressure. He wouldn't really do it, but this guy didn't know that.

"You can't," the man squealed. "I got rights."

"I'm not a cop. Just a friendly neighbor who doesn't mind using your fragile little bones to find out the information I need to protect this nice lady."

Eva hurried back out the patio door with a coiled rope.

"Ryken is who paid me," the man screamed.

"Ryken?" Eva repeated. "Not Jorge?"

"Who's Jorge?" the perp asked. Miles wondered the same thing. Did she have a stalker?

Miles released some of the intense pressure on the guy's arm. "What did he pay you to do?"

"Just scare her."

"You are a liar and a brute," Eva said, handing the rope to Miles. "You tried to suffocate me."

"I would've stopped when you passed out."

Miles glanced up at Eva. Her face said she didn't believe the guy. He didn't know if he did either. Just scare her? That was risky, and dumb. Eva would have cameras and a security system. He wasn't wearing a mask or gloves. He'd definitely be apprehended and prosecuted for attacking her.

"We'll chat more in a second," Miles said.

Then he went to work, roping the guy like he would a five-hundred-pound steer. The man squealed and protested and squirmed, but he was no match for Miles. He'd never roped professionally like Walker, but he could hold his own.

Finished, he stood and turned to Eva. Her eyes were wide. She looked from him down to her attacker and back up. "You trussed him up like roping a steer," she said, her admiration evident. "Faster than Cole Patterson."

It was a conscious effort not to puff out his chest. Cole Patterson was a legend. "I did the rodeo circuit in high school."

"Where are you from?" she asked.

"Montana."

"Back up the bus! I'm from Wyoming."

"I know." He smiled at her. If anyone would've told him he'd be having a normal conversation with Eva Chevron after rescuing her from an attacker, he would've told *them* to 'back up the bus'.

"You know who I am?" Her face pinched, and she clung to the back of a patio chair. Was she feeling dizzy?

"Are you all right?" He stepped closer.

"Fine." She held up a hand. "Please answer the question."

"I might be a military man, but they do allow us Wi-Fi." He

grinned. "I'd have to live under a rock to not know who Eva Chevron is."

She didn't answer but focused on the man glaring up at them from the concrete.

"Apologies," Miles murmured. Their connection was suddenly spiraling into the atmosphere. Was she as humble as she was brave? "Did you not want me to know who you were?"

"It's fine. It's just ..." She licked her lips. "I imagined when you were running and smiled at me that you were interested in me ... not my famous status."

"Eva," Miles started to protest, but then the words died on his lips. Everything he saw or read about her was incredible, but he didn't know the real her. How could he? They'd just met. He could completely understand why she didn't want someone interested in her because of her fame. "It's not like that," he began, but he didn't know what to say. What was it like? He was just another admirer. They didn't have some special connection like he'd imagined from the first and second looks and smiles, and, an annoying voice reminded him, he had a responsibility to break up with Lily before he could go hitting on any woman.

"It's fine," she rushed out. She turned and picked up her phone. "I'll call the police." She pressed a hand to her forehead and sighed. "Actually, I'm supposed to call my FBI agent first." Instead of dialing, she kept staring at the phone. "Agent Ryken Henderson."

Miles straightened and an uneasy quiver turned his stomach. "Pardon me?"

She met his gaze. "Do you think that's a coincidence?"

"Unusual name," he muttered, glancing down at the perp, then around at the night shadows. "What's Ryken's last name?" he asked the tied-up man.

"How should I know?" the guy muttered. "He left money and instructions for me, is all. I got no last name, number, or anything. I shouldn't even know his name, but I'm smart and I scouted out the meeting spot early. I overheard his buddy calling him Ryken. I was early today too, took out the patio camera and sneaked up on her." He was proud of himself, obviously. "I don't trust Ryken not to double-cross me and try to get me arrested or something."

Was that why Ryken wasn't here yet? Miles didn't trust this guy's bragging. "What did Ryken look like?" He pressed.

"It was dark. I never got a clear look at his face. Dark hair, black suit."

Miles looked to Eva. She shivered. "Ryken has dark hair."

Of course he'd wear a suit if he was an agent. The urgency to get Eva far from here increased. A couple more quick questions.

"Did you come from the beach or the front of the house?" Miles asked.

"Through the house. I had the code to disable the alarms."

Eva startled and backed up a step. "How did you get my code?"

"The note from Ryken," he said.

Miles's gut churned. "Who knows your code?"

"My parents. My FBI agent, Ryken Henderson. He helped the security people install the best system."

Bile climbed his throat. None of this was sitting well.

Eva focused the power of those dark eyes on him. She looked vulnerable and uncertain. He was a natural protector of women and children. It had been taught to him from toddlerhood on up. His experiences in far-flung countries with the military, where often women and children had no rights, had reinforced those instincts. Looking at Eva right now, every protective instinct in his body fired. He would protect her from this Ryken and any other idiot who tried to hurt or scare her.

He almost stepped to her and enfolded her in his arms, but he didn't know how she'd receive that, and they didn't have time for reassurances or the bond he longed to forge with her.

"I'm sure it's not the same person." Eva worried her lip. "But …"

"If there's a chance, you shouldn't call that agent," he finished for her.

What if the guy had set this all up for some sick reason? To be the hero? To get a ransom? Who knew? This Ryken might be on his way. He might be here already.

"Eva." He swallowed hard. He didn't want to scare her, but if Ryken was here or coming, they needed some distance. "Let's walk out on the beach a bit."

She didn't look like she wanted to leave her house, but she nodded and strode off the patio.

"I wouldn't go screaming for help if I were you," he said to the attacker. "I imagine you've got a long rap sheet and if you scream and the police come running, they aren't going to go easy on the man that tried to kill Eva Chevron." Miles needed some time to figure this out and the guy was going nowhere tied like he was.

The man's mouth went slack. "I didn't try to kill her."

Miles ignored him and followed Eva. They walked out to the water and then turned back to face her house. The house and others around it were lit up. With the sun gone, the beach and ocean were dark. He half-expected 'Ryken' to come prowling after them.

"I know you don't know me from Adam," he said to Eva, "but …" He hated name dropping and bragging, but he needed her to trust him so he could protect her. "I'm friends with Captain Aiden Porter and Lieutenant Quaid Raven. I served with Quaid. Do you know them?"

Her brows lifted. "I know their reputations. Aiden Porter has a house a couple miles up the beach."

"That's where I ran from. I'm staying there."

"Impressive friends. Are you trying to brag?"

His neck felt hot. He rubbed at it. "You're Eva Chevron. My friends wouldn't impress you."

She folded her arms across her chest and shrugged. Since he'd told her he knew her, she hadn't been as warm or flirtatious.

"Why did you name drop then?" she asked.

"This feels really off to me. If this Ryken is your agent and he paid this guy to attack you ..." He shook his head. "I don't know. I'm wondering if he orchestrated it all and is going to show up and play the hero, or maybe he was planning to kidnap you for ransom or trafficking."

She shivered and stepped closer to him. "But he couldn't have orchestrated all the messages from Jorge Augilar from prison and being personally assigned to my case."

Something about Jorge Augilar tickled at his mind, but if the man was in prison, he wasn't the most immediate issue. "Does Agent Henderson hit on you?"

She gave him a look as if trying to decide how to answer such an obtuse question.

"Okay, sorry. I'm sure every man hits on you. Have you turned him down for a date?"

She nodded.

Miles didn't like any of this. They had to get out of here, get Eva to a safe place, and figure out where to go from there.

"Would you be opposed to walking down the beach with me to Aiden's house? We can call Aiden as we walk, get some inside information on Agent Ryken Henderson. If he's clean, Aiden's people will verify it. Maybe Jorge knows Ryken is your agent and is trying to make you not trust him by hiring some guy to attack you. You think Jorge would have those kinds of connections from prison?"

"Yes." But she didn't sound convinced that was the answer. "Should I just leave everything?"

"Yes. If Ryken isn't a threat, you'll be back."

They turned and walked together. He appreciated that she trusted him enough to listen and come with him. He wouldn't have left her here alone if she'd refused to come with him, but getting entangled with a dirty FBI agent couldn't end well.

Eva glanced back. "Isn't it a crime to leave a crime scene?"

He smiled. "We'll be okay. If everything checks out, we'll be back soon."

"Thank you." She glanced up at him. Even in the semi-dark, her face was more beautiful than anything he'd ever seen, and he'd seen Montana sunsets. "You don't even know me and you're helping me. Well, I guess you *think* you know me."

Miles had no idea how to respond to that. Hollywood relationships must be a nightmare, cutting through the public persona and finding the real person underneath. Not his issue right now. His attraction to Eva had to be thrown to the rear seat of the bus as well.

He pulled out his phone to call Aiden when suddenly a voice called from behind them and to their right, "Eva?" A beat, then louder, "Eva!"

Eva stiffened and backed away from the man calling from her patio. Miles pocketed his phone, almost reaching for his gun.

Together they eased farther down the beach, watching him. The man searched the dark night but didn't seem to see them.

When they had about a hundred feet of distance and were shrouded by the dark night, Miles saw the man bend down to the attacker.

He took Eva's hand, and they raced together away from her home and whoever that guy was.

The fact that she clung to his hand and ran as fast as he could told him the man looking for her wasn't a friend.

CHAPTER
Three

EVA RACED with Miles along the beach. Her head hurt, but she ignored it. A rock or seashell occasionally poked at her bare feet, but she wasn't about to complain.

She panted for air and held onto Miles's hand like a lifeline. Talk about sent straight from heaven. Miles wasn't flashy or a bragger, even though he was obviously the toughest man she'd ever met in real life. When all Eva wanted to do was freak out, he seemed to be built for situations like this.

Agent Ryken Henderson had been on her back patio. What did that mean? Was he the bad guy? Could he really have set up an attacker to get her to turn to him as the rescuing hero?

He hadn't looked in their direction, but who knew if the sound of their running had given them away? Or if he would come down to the beach to look for footprints leading away. She was trusting Miles, a man she'd just met, over the FBI agent who'd helped install her security system. Was she acting nuts? Her dad always told her to trust the Spirit. She prayed in her head as they ran and didn't see any stop signs, so she kept running. Miles's confidence, competence, and the bond she'd instantly felt with her 'fantasy running man' who'd become her rescuer strengthened her.

The Balboa Pier was just in front of them. It was lit up and people were walking along it to the restaurant. Miles pulled her into the rolling water and under the darkness of the pier. They went behind one of the huge wooden posts and then he tugged her to a stop.

"You all right?" he asked.

"I feel like a hen who's lost her roost."

He chuckled softly at that. "You sure are brave," he said. The admiration in his voice felt all directed at her bravery, nothing to do with her fame.

She was out of breath, didn't know that she was acting brave or just reacting. She wasn't sure of anything at the moment. She'd acted as a tough female warrior, Charli, in *Protecting the Heiress*. She tried to channel those vibes and be as brave as Miles thought she was.

A wave broke on their legs, dousing her up to her waist with salty and chilly liquid. She shivered. It may be the first of August, but the California ocean water was cold all year long. Some of the scrapes the attacker had given her stung from the salt water.

A rough-looking man eased around one of the other posts. Eva let out a squeak of surprise.

Miles stepped in front of her and pulled a pistol from the back waistband of his pants. She hadn't even realized he was armed.

"You don't want to mess with us," Miles said in a low warning growl.

Eva hadn't seen such an appealing picture in many years, or maybe she had. The first moment she and Miles's gazes had connected earlier tonight was as appealing. That couldn't factor in right now. She was in danger and Miles was protecting her. She had to face reality. This wasn't a movie, and he wasn't her soul mate. He'd simply been intrigued by meeting the famous actress, like most of the male population. She couldn't let herself think it was more, then be devastated when he was just another guy wanting to have his shot with a celebrity, another handsome face who would move on when a better option appeared.

"Sheesh, man." The guy put up his hands. "I was just looking for a buck or two."

"I only carry weapons, not money," Miles said evenly.

"Psycho." The guy turned and walked the other direction.

Miles turned back to her. She almost collapsed against him. He was the brave one and could give any actor lessons in magnetism, appeal, courage, and heroism.

Before she could fling herself at his very appealing chest, he said in whisper, "Flatten against the post."

She trusted Miles. He had the cowboy and military vibe down to an art. Maybe she should question why she instinctively trusted him. Instead, she obeyed.

The post smelled of mildew and dead fish and was slimy and covered with barnacles. Miles pressed in behind her. His warm, strong body overshadowed and protected her. No matter what was coming at them, she was safe with this military cowboy. A few moments passed with the waves rhythmically breaking against them and her unable to catch her breath. From the sprint, the fear, the attack, or was it all Miles's appeal making her lack oxygen?

"Where's your phone?" he whispered in her ear.

She pulled it out of the pocket of her shorts and handed it to him.

"Don't move."

He edged away from her, and Eva wanted to follow him. It was instinctive to want to stay close. He went deeper into the water and to the other edge of the wide pier. Then he chucked her phone up and onto the pier.

"Hey!" a male voice called. "A phone ... sweet!" Footsteps raced across the wooden pier above their heads and toward the Peninsula Park and Balboa Fun Zone that was east of the pier.

Eva couldn't believe he'd just thrown her phone to somebody. What was he thinking? She didn't dare move or holler at him, or at the kid who'd rushed off with her iPhone. Could the kick unlock it and get her banking information, passwords to everything, and plenty of fodder to sell to the paparazzi?

Miles worked his way silently through the waves until he surrounded her with his body and she was pushed against the slimy, rough wooden piling again.

"What are you doing?" she dared ask.

"Somebody's coming right at us, slowly closing in from the south. I can see his shadow and part of his face with a lit-up phone screen he's holding. It looks like the guy who called to you from your patio. There might be a tracker in your phone that would lead him straight to us."

Eva's stomach turned over. Was there a tracker on her phone? Ryken and Lake had both taken her phone at different times in the last week. Could one of them have installed a tracker? What if Ryken was in league with Jorge? Was the dangerous criminal Jorge even after her, or was that a ploy like the man attacking her tonight to give Ryken an in with her? To make a play for her, ransom her, or traffic her like Miles had said? Were there other options? She was confused, scared, and out of her element. Real life was not supposed to mirror movie scripts.

She froze and waited for a word or signal from Miles. Even the waves rushing against her legs, the smelly post she was pressed against, and the fear of Ryken being a bad guy and tracking them down couldn't distract from the warmth and safety that Miles offered her.

"Let's go," Miles said. "He headed east. It looks like he's following the kid who ran off with your phone up into the amusement park."

Again, Miles had been right. His quick thinking had saved her more than once tonight. Apparently his life did mimic a cloak and dagger script, because he was rolling with all of this insanity as if it was a Tuesday morning at the office. What kind of soldier was he?

He eased back, took her hand, and led her out from under the pier to the north. They stayed in the water for a while, then he angled up to the sand. He kept checking to the east and south.

"Can you double-time again?" he asked.

"Sure."

They upped their pace to a fast jog, not quite as fast as their sprint earlier. Eva's head started to pound again, but she refused to say anything about it. She was alive and safe. She could deal with a lingering headache.

Miles released her hand so they could both use their arms to pump and get into a rhythmic run in the harder packed sand by the water's edge. It didn't escape her attention that Miles edged her toward the most level and hard-packed sand while he took the more difficult route in the softer sand.

Eva didn't love running, but her personal trainer Darlene put her through running and sprinting drills often. She'd run to save her own life. It felt like hours later but was probably less than half an hour that Miles slowed to a stop and directed her up the beach through the soft sand and toward a staircase.

The landscape had changed from the flat beach outside her house's rear windows to a sharp bluff with homes perched above the sand and ocean. Eva was famous and doing well financially, but these homes belonged to the ultra-wealthy and infamous. People like Aiden Porter.

They stopped in front of the house she'd learned was Aiden and Chalisa Porter's. Miles gestured, and she preceded him up the stairs. There was a locked gate at the top. He eased in front of her, brushing his chest against her shoulder and sending her pulse racing. She ignored the sensation. Miles was helping and protecting her, and that had to be all. She appreciated his help and kept praying she was making the right choice by trusting him and not Ryken. He just … felt right, but wouldn't it be a kick in the teeth if Miles somehow wasn't the trustworthy one? She'd chosen wrong with every boyfriend since leaving home ten years ago.

Miles typed in a code and the gate lock beeped. He held it open for her, glancing around the dark, quiet beach before following her through and shutting the gate.

They walked onto a gorgeous patio area with a pool glowing blue in the night, low lights around the pool and throughout the flower beds. The scents of chlorine mingled with eucalyptus, gardenia, and orange.

Miles directed her around the pool and to an outdoor shower. They both rinsed off their legs and feet of sand and salt water. He pulled two beach towels out of a cabinet underneath the outdoor kitchen set against the far side of the patio. She dried her feet and legs, her skin no longer stinging from the salt water, except where she had scrapes from her attacker. Squeezing the moisture out of her shorts, she could see Miles doing the same.

Her hands trembled. It made sense that she'd be full of adrenaline after the attack and their escape, but was she also slightly apprehensive about being alone with Miles? She glanced at him. His handsome face turned toward her—serious, protective, appealing. Could she trust him?

He took her towel from her hand, brushing his fingers against hers. She trembled even more from that simple touch. If he wasn't trustworthy, her radar was way off. He felt like a guy from home and the most enticing military hero and cowboy combined. He appeared genuine with no need to brag about himself or 'charm' her like most men did.

Giving her an endearing and almost awkward smile at their brushing of fingers, he dropped the towels in a bin, then typed in another code and opened a French door. He gestured for her to walk in first.

She should be leery, walking into a quiet house with a stranger, a man who'd thrown her cell phone away. Her Fitbit didn't make calls or send messages. She'd had to get rid of her Apple Watch to get a break from all the emails, texts, and phone calls and give her mind some down time.

Instead of feeling apprehensive, she felt ... welcomed and safe. Was that the feeling in Aiden Porter's house or was that all Miles?

Still, her dad would not appreciate her lack of caution. "How do I know you're who you say you are and didn't stage my attacker so you could rescue me, toss my phone away, bring me here, and take advantage of Eva Chevron?"

"Um ..." Miles's eyes widened. "Well ... do you want to see my identification or call Aiden or Quaid on my phone?"

She bit her lip. His eyes fell to her mouth and stayed there. A thrill went through her. She pushed it away. It had been a bizarre night, and she needed to somehow think about this logically. He could have numbers listed in his phone as Aiden Porter and Quaid Raven.

"Do you have ID?"

"Not on me. I was running." He lifted his hands. "Do you want to wait while I grab my wallet?"

"Yes, please."

He nodded to her. She couldn't tell if he was annoyed that she wasn't fully trusting him. He didn't seem to be, but it was hard to tell with the stoic military type. Interesting that he didn't carry his wallet while running but he hadn't left his pistol behind.

He walked into the house. She stood in the open patio door, half in and half out. If he'd had evil intent, wouldn't he have simply yanked her inside? He could close the door and she'd be caught.

She didn't like the doubts or her fears, but she had to be smart and leery.

Leery was hard to dredge up when she thought of how Miles focused his brilliantly blue eyes on her. She bit her lip and waited impatiently for him. She could do without the fears and attack of tonight, but she didn't know how she'd go back to life before Miles. His blue eyes and the instant draw to him brought a sparkle to her life she hadn't realized was missing.

Please let Miles be as genuine and loyal as he appears, she prayed.

CHAPTER Four

MILES REAPPEARED with a wallet and pulled out a few cards, handing them over to her.

"Thank you." She looked at his driver's license. She'd been right—six-four, two-twenty. Nice stats. "You are a dead ringer for Miles Coleville."

"I hope so." He folded his arms across his chest, and she found herself temporarily distracted.

Glancing away quickly, she turned to his military ID. A lieutenant in the Navy. Wow, that was even more impressive. He had also handed her an outdated card for the Northern Rodeo Association. "Glad you have proof that you are a roper."

He smirked at that. "Didn't want you to think I was lying about any of it."

"I'm sorry. I didn't mean to intone … Everything just happened so fast, and I instinctively trusted you, but … With me being famous and maybe you orchestrated the attack and the rescue like we think Ryken did." She broke off at the tightening around his mouth. "A girl can never be too careful. Sorry, I'll stop talking now." She handed the cards back, ignoring the rush from his fingertips touching hers.

She'd just made a fool of herself. She wasn't caught up in her fame, but she hadn't met a man in years who wasn't awed by her fame or wanting to use it to benefit him.

"No. You don't need to apologize." He put the cards in and then put his wallet in his pocket. "I'm grateful you're being cautious. It did all happen fast, and I should've found a way to reassure you more. I was focused on keeping you safe, but I'm incredibly impressed with how brave you have been."

"Ah." She put a hand to her heart. "That means a lot." Coming from this specimen of rescue hero, it really did. "You did reassure me. You're a poster for tough, honorable, military cowboys. I'm impressed and grateful. Thank you. For everything."

Now she was gushing. It wasn't to make up for doubting him; she felt all of it and wondered more with each passing moment if her first impression hadn't been dead on and this was the man she should've been looking for all her life. He'd not only found her but rescued her.

"It's nothing," he murmured softly.

Their gazes caught and held. Blue eyes like his didn't capture a girl every day. She'd seen a lot of handsome men in Hollywood. Miles was more than handsome. He was real, could tease with her, protect her, and though he seemed humble and drawn to her, he was confident enough to stand by her side, not be tongue-tied or grasping at her fame.

"We'd better get inside," Miles said. "We weren't followed, but better not to be where someone could get a glimpse of Eva Chevron."

His words broke the spell. Probably for the best. She wanted to be safe, and she was moving much too fast with him, at least in her own head.

She walked over the threshold. Miles followed her, shut the door, and pressed a button to re-arm the security.

"Somebody's serious about their security, eh?"

He smirked. "It's Aiden Porter. This is the smallest of his homes, with the least gadgets. You should try to get into his headquarters. He puts a survivalist hiding from the Russian mafia to shame."

She barked a loud laugh at that.

Miles grinned.

Did he think her barking laugh was obnoxious? Lake had. She looked around. There were only accent lights on above the cabinets and high shelves and some lamps, but she could see a spacious living area with loads of windows, especially behind them overlooking the pool area and ocean.

"Could somebody see in?" She pointed at the patio doors and floor to ceiling windows.

"Tinted glass and bulletproof." He winked.

"The second top security specialist in the world thinks of everything. Aiden is like James Bond, Ethan Hunt, and Jason Bourne put together."

"Careful. It'll go to his head."

"You're going to repeat everything I say?"

"No. The thing you don't see are all the cameras recording everything we say and do." Miles lifted a hand, gesturing around the spacious room. "I was telling you I'd call him, but if I were a betting man, that comment will get us …" As if on cue, he pulled out his phone. He had it on silent, but the screen was lit up with a picture of the handsome, charming Aiden Porter.

"Aiden," Miles greeted him as if they were close friends. If Miles was staying at his house, he was closer to the charming Aiden Porter than most who claimed to be his best friend. Miles didn't seem to know the meaning of posturing. She loved that.

"Yes, Eva Chevron did just walk into your house with me." He smiled at Eva. "No, she's not here as my date. She's in trouble."

Eva studied Miles's face as he explained everything that had happened to her tonight to *the* Aiden Porter. Surreal. This entire night and that she was standing in Aiden Porter's home. She might be famous, but Aiden was legendary. Miles being friends with and staying in Aiden Porter's house was no small matter. She was grateful for Miles's connections and willingness to help her. A notorious friend like Aiden Porter made Eva think that Miles might not be star-struck by her. He might be interested in the real her like those lingering blue-eyed glances were saying, and not just after her because she was famous.

Miles put the phone on speaker.

"Eva," Aiden said. "Welcome to our home."

"Thank you." She assumed he meant his gorgeous wife Chalisa Anderson Porter, sister to Princess Reagan Anderson Magnum as the 'our.'

"Lieutenant Miles Coleville is a trustworthy and impressive man, but you probably already know that."

Miles ducked his head slightly. Was he actually humble too? Had the good Lord created her perfect man? She'd prayed and Miles had appeared. Her body tingled at the thought. She might be in grave danger, but the gift of Miles in her life would be worth finding out her FBI agent wasn't a good guy. Especially if Aiden could fix it all and she could be back to work and her house come morning.

"I learned that firsthand tonight," she admitted.

"Are you comfortable waiting at my home alone with Miles until we get a take on this situation and this Agent Henderson, or would you prefer I have one of my operatives in the area come for you? I'd trust Miles with Chalisa's life and he's as tough and well-trained as my people, but I realize you don't know him and you are Eva Chevron. I swear to you I'll have a security turret drop from the ceiling and shoot Miles in the hand if he tries to get too friendly."

She barked a laugh at that surprising line. Especially as Aiden had said it with all his characteristic charm.

Miles smiled, but then he held her gaze. His enticing blue eyes asked her to wait with him, to get to know him better and see where it could lead. She knew little about him besides that he was a military cowboy, but she trusted him. He'd fought for her, hidden her, protected her in every way.

"I'm comfortable with Miles," she admitted.

"Perfect. Thank you. Now, Miles. In the master suite, there are plenty of Chalisa's clothing that will fit Eva and toiletries or anything else she might need."

Eva didn't want to take Chalisa Porter's clothing. She hoped they could sort out this mess and she could be back home well before she needed clothing or toiletries. She wasn't on location, but they were filming some wrap-up scenes at the studio for her latest movie. As soon as she got that done, she could fly to Wyoming. She couldn't hide out here infinitely. Even if the mesmerizing Miles Coleville was by her side.

"Thank you," she said rather than express all her concerns and timelines. Better to see what they found out. But there was something she and Miles had forgotten. "Miles didn't tell you, but can you also look into Jorge Augilar? He became obsessed with me two weeks ago, apparently after he saw *The Broken Warrior* in prison." The film was adapted from a Taylor Hart novel. It was a couple years old and used to be one of her favorites, with action, intrigue, and romance. Jorge had ruined that for her. "He sends me messages from prison constantly."

"Jorge Augilar?" Aiden repeated. "I put him in prison. He tried to take advantage of Chalisa." His voice was as hard as she'd ever heard it. But then she'd only heard him in interviews when he was delighting a talk show host with witty banter.

"Ryken told me you did," she admitted.

"Interesting. This Ryken is a name-dropper, eh?"

Eva looked to Miles. She'd accused him of being a name-dropper when he told her he knew Aiden Porter and Quaid Raven.

"He likes to brag, that's for sure." She realized with the suspicious light now cast on Ryken that she had appreciated but never relaxed around her FBI agent. She'd thought that was because he had hit on her and asked her out, but maybe it was something deeper. Was Ryken a bad guy, a schemer trying to get a famous actress to like and trust him, or was he a pawn for Jorge?

"Sounds like an odd flex, telling a target inside information. I will definitely check into Jorge. Maybe even pay him a visit in prison." Aiden sounded like he would enjoy that. "Did Agent Henderson always come alone?"

"Yes. Is that wrong?"

"FBI agents can work alone, but in the field they typically have a partner. It seems as if he wanted you all to himself."

A shiver went down her spine. It seemed she was lucky Ryken hadn't done anything to her before now. If this was all his doing.

"Agent Henderson also helped her install her security system," Miles put in. "I didn't share that earlier."

"Even more interesting. But he didn't recommend you hire private security or relocate to a gated and secure community?" Aiden asked.

"No. My agent did. I was planning to look into it after I returned from Wyoming. I had plans to visit my family after we finished filming."

"Hmm. I'll be in touch soon," Aiden said. "Thank you, Miles. I'm certain Eva feels the same, but I'm grateful you happened upon her tonight."

"Me too," Miles and Eva said at the same time.

Aiden laughed at that, and she smiled, embarrassed.

"Aiden," Miles said, thankfully interrupting her embarrassment. "I chucked her phone onto the pier and some kid took off with it. I think this Ryken was tracking her with it. Can you have one of your tech people kill it so nobody can get her information from it?"

Eva appreciated him dealing with that concern as well.

"Of course. Phone number? Carrier?"

Eva rattled both off.

"Got it. All right, hang tight." Aiden hung up, and silence filled the large living space.

Miles pocketed his phone, pivoting slightly. Eva stared at the gun tucked in the back of his waistband and asked, "Why didn't you just beat up Ryken or threaten him with the gun? Why did we run?" Running had felt like the right move to her, but she didn't have fighting skills like Miles did.

"If your FBI agent really is dirty, we need answers before I show him my face. I could either get arrested for thumping an FBI agent or lose the anonymity I currently have. I told you my name while the attacker was passed out and only my first name. Whoever's after you won't know who's protecting you. Especially since your attacker said he took out the patio camera."

She stared at him for a beat. "So you're not just a tough, handsome cowboy lieutenant. You're a thinker too?"

He grinned and her insides did a happy dance. "I am a SEAL. They expect us to think, not just be tough."

"You're ... a Navy SEAL." She moistened her lips. "That is even more impressive."

He ducked his head slightly. "Forgive me. My mama would not like me bragging."

"You weren't bragging." He became more impressive and appealing by the moment.

He arched an eyebrow. "Would you like to shower or change your clothes? Do you want something to eat or drink?"

The redirection was intriguing and disappointing. She hadn't let down her guard around a man since she had finally broken free of Lake last year. Miles had acted enthralled with her when they first met, but now he seemed to be withdrawing.

"I'll stay in my clothes until we know I can't go back to my house tonight," she said.

Both eyebrows lifted at that. He didn't think she'd be returning anytime soon. Was Ryken a 'dirty' agent? The thought blew her mind, but she also realized how gullible she'd been if he was. She'd let him set up her security and been alone with him.

"Some ice water and Tylenol would be fabulous, and I'd love to use a restroom to wash up."

"Your head." He shook his own head. "I'm sorry. I forgot in all the uproar. The perp knocking you around and knocking you out must've hurt, and coming to after being unconscious is vicious. You are very brave." He didn't wait for her response, rushing into the kitchen area to open a cupboard.

She followed him. He opened a bottle of Tylenol, cupped his free hand under hers, and tilted a couple pills into her palm.

Eva was frozen by the warm pressure of his hand cupping hers. No, frozen wasn't right. She was warm all over. Miles's blue eyes met hers and all the danger, uncertainty, and worries disappeared. Nothing could ever go wrong. There was no danger in this world. If he was close by.

He surprised her when he stepped back, slid his hand away, and refastened the pill bottle lid. He put it back in the cabinet and shut the door, then hurried to another cabinet, grabbed a glass, and went to the fridge to fill it with ice and water.

Eva watched him. Was she misreading the signals he had given before or was he interested in her? She hadn't met a single man in years who hadn't either acted awkward in her presence, 'preened like a peacock' in her dad's words, or made a play for her. She knew they were after her because of her fame, not anything to do with the real her.

Miles confused her. She'd never been drawn to a man like this. It could be argued her attraction was simply gratitude for her rescuer or because he wasn't hitting on her nonstop, chasing her like most other men did. He was a brave, tough cowboy and Navy SEAL, protecting and taking tender care of her. That could be why he was irresistible.

Yet she felt like they had something more between them than a hero complex or him playing hard to get. Something deep and promising. In this temporary safe haven of Aiden Porter's home, could she explore this interest in Miles and see if he returned it?

He walked over with the glass of water and offered it to her.

Eva murmured her thanks and took it from him, brushing his fingers in the process.

He sucked in a breath and didn't move. Eva placed the Tylenol on her tongue and then took a long drink of the water. Miles watched her mouth the entire time. She shouldn't have done it, but she let a drop of water roll slowly over her bottom lip. The water clung to her lip, and she figured, why not? She gave him a 'come hither' glance with her eyes, lowering her eyelashes and looking up from underneath them.

Her parents would be appalled at the 'seductive moves' she'd learned from many a role, but her sisters would cheer. Especially if they could see this handsome cowboy and Navy SEAL lieutenant who'd rescued her. Eva was slightly embarrassed that she was using tricks from her acting career to draw this man in, but she owed him at least a hug of thanks, if not one sweet kiss.

She waited, and Miles took the bait. He eased closer and touched the moisture with the pad of his thumb. Eva sucked in a breath at the feeling of his touch just below her lip. Then he took it to the next step, trailing his thumb up and over her lower lip.

She felt like she had entered the romance scene of an action movie. On screen, it was all business and no real feeling. Right now, she experienced every feel. Miles's touch, Miles's heated gaze, Miles's large frame overshadowing her. His touch was magical, better than anything actors could try to replicate. She'd never been part of such a slow, tender moment. Most men came at her hard and fast, thinking they could get her to like them if they went at her with gusto.

Miles was in no rush. She'd never met a hero the likes of this guy. Maybe what she'd been doing wrong was dating celebrities. She should've been looking for a military cowboy. Not just any military cowboy. Only Miles would do for her.

Her lip trembled under his touch.

"Eva," he murmured in a husky groan, his blue eyes deepening to a smolder that made her heart race out of control.

She set the glass on the counter and slid her hands across his muscular shoulders, and he let out a soft, telling moan. He cupped her jawline with his large palm and continued to gently trace her lower lip. Her mouth parted in anticipation, waiting for him to replace his thumb with his lips and create unparalleled sparks. They would deepen this bond between them, and she would relish every moment.

Miles didn't kiss her. He studied her, as if checking for sincerity, or maybe he was too much of a gentleman to kiss a woman he hardly knew, and a famous woman at that. She wanted the man she fell for to want her for her, not because she was famous. Miles had known who she was, probably from the first look as he was running. She hadn't liked that, but it wasn't his fault. They'd only met an hour ago, and he'd done everything to protect her and help her, with no thought of reward.

She was ready to give him a kiss of gratitude, but he wasn't complying.

Arching up onto tiptoes, she slid her hands up and around his neck, threading them along his scalp and eliciting another groan. His hand came around her neck, into her hair, and created the most incredible sensation as he gently massaged her scalp.

His other hand cupped her waist and hip, bringing her body flush against his.

Eva was on fire and looking forward to a better kiss than she'd ever experienced in her life. When he still didn't bend down to kiss her, she moistened her lips again and said, "Is it out of line to give you a kiss of gratitude for rescuing me?"

His body stiffened against her, and he said in a rush, "Eva ... you have no idea how badly I want to kiss you right now, but ..."

Eva liked everything about his sentence. Except for the but. She waited. He didn't continue. Was she acting too forward? She spoke her mind and was bold, but she'd never had to beg for a kiss before.

"But you're protecting me?" she guessed.

He swallowed and nodded.

She fell back onto her heels, disappointed.

"And there's a girl back home ..." He took a deep breath. "Ah, man."

"Sheesh!" She ripped herself away from his grasp and knocked the glass of water over. "Dang it all to heck!"

Miles righted the glass before she could and grabbed some paper towels, mopping up the mess.

Eva backed away and watched him, pressing the heel of her hand into her forehead. She'd forgotten all about her headache while he touched her and she anticipated his kiss, but now it came back full force. What had she been thinking? What had he?

A girl back home? Someone he'd always loved? A committed relationship or simply the girl he'd never been able to forget? Was Miles a two-timing jerk? She'd been around far too many actors who insisted they could 'hook up' while on location and then go back to their respective spouses and girlfriends. She'd had fans and even stalkers who claimed she was the love of their lives and that they were ditching their spouses for her. She wanted no part in such immoral exchanges. She wanted real, devoted, loyal.

And this five-minutes-ago-perfect-to-her man ... Miles had protected her, made her feel special. She'd never experienced a connection and draw like this. The cowboy and Navy SEAL lieutenant coming on to her while he had a committed girl waiting for him? It didn't fit.

Was this all about her making the moves on him, pushing him when he wasn't interested? Yet he'd held her hand, touched her, protected her, given her those longing looks.

She hung her head. She'd obviously been seeing it all wrong. Miles had been taking care of her and being a gentleman, not hitting on her. It wasn't like they'd had a lot of time to talk about ... anything. She barely knew his name; she was the one making a mess of this situation. She felt more sympathy for the men who'd hit on her when she wasn't interested. This was more awkward than a cow in a prom dress from the pursuer's standpoint.

"Excuse me," she murmured. "I'll just ... use the restroom." She looked around, but all she saw was the massive great room, some stairs, and a loft area above them.

Miles glanced at her, his hands full of wet paper towels. He looked somber and regretful. Maybe he wished he didn't have a girlfriend or a 'girl back home', whatever that meant. It didn't matter. She wasn't into two-timing. She'd heard lewd comments such as, 'My wife would understand, since you're my hall pass,' from male fans, and 'What happens on location stays on location' from fellow actors. Such sentiments were disgusting, immoral, and unacceptable. Miles would never be gross like those men. She'd instigated the exchange, and he could have easily kissed her. The fact that he was loyal to his Montana girl made her respect him, and made him off-limits.

He pointed. "There's a bathroom off the garage or four bathrooms attached to each of the suites downstairs. Upstairs is the master where Chalisa's clothes and toiletries would be."

She nodded, dodged to the stairs, and pumped up them. She wasn't going to change her clothes and get comfortable, but she wouldn't mind washing up and using some lotion.

"Wait, please."

She whirled halfway up the stairs. Miles climbed the stairs and stopped just below her. His blue eyes consumed her. She wrapped her hands around the railing behind her and pressed back against it, determined not to reach for him. He was faithful to his 'girl back home'. As he should be.

"I know Aiden's house is secure, but I don't want to take any risks. Let me do a sweep."

"Oh." Even though she'd been determined not to reach for him, it still stung that he hadn't come after her to explain about the girl. Maybe he'd thought he loved the girl from home, until he touched Eva, and now he knew who his soulmate was.

She nodded and looked away, embarrassed. Was she trying to steal Miles now? She wasn't some boyfriend stealer. And if Miles decided he didn't want his girl because he had a more famous option, just as Lake last year and a dozen other boyfriends earlier in her career had done to her, she would lose all respect for him.

She could feel Miles's gaze on her, but she did not look up.

He ascended the stairs, and she waited, clutching the railing and pettily wishing she didn't know about the other girl. This perfect hero she'd built up in her mind and fallen for the past hour as he protected and helped her was definitely not her match. She appreciated his loyalty and integrity to his girl, and it made him off limits.

A drug lord was obsessed with her from prison. An FBI

agent might be misusing his power to get her attention or, worse, be working for Jorge. She'd been attacked and knocked out by a vicious brute.

Despite all of that, all she could focus on was Miles not being her dream man.

Depressed wasn't strong enough. Mortified might fit. Devastated was even better.

Tonight had morphed from a romantic suspense with hope of the hero saving the day and winning the heroine's heart to a horror movie where every likeable character died.

CHAPTER *Five*

MILES CHECKED THE MASTER SUITE, stewing about the mess he'd created. He could've smacked himself upside the head. He'd been inches from kissing Eva, the most incredible woman he'd ever met, and he'd tried to explain about Lily. Easton and Walker would attempt to thrash him for missing the opportunity of a lifetime. The two of them together might accomplish it.

He and Lily hadn't had much of a relationship for years now. He hadn't spoken to her or texted her in … at least two months. She usually waited for him to reach out in case he was on a mission, and he hadn't felt any urge to reach out since the awkwardness of their last date. The only thing standing between him not having any commitment to Lily was a one-on-one conversation.

If only he'd been more determined to make a clean break six months ago. He'd felt like the worst of human refuse when Lily started crying. It wasn't like her to turn on the waterworks so he'd known she was genuinely distressed. Now as he thought about those tears, he wondered if something else was going on that had nothing to do with him or their relationship.

After an hour of being around Eva, he could easily see that his and Lily's 'love' was a high school relationship that should've ended long ago. Any romantic feelings had burned out. Their friendship remained, but them 'dating' seemed more of a title to him.

He'd kept himself busy with the SEALs and hadn't dated anyone but Lily. What did a teenager, then a man wholly focused on becoming a world-class soldier, know about love? Though he'd known they had little hope of a future, he'd remained loyal to Lily. Right now, he felt anything but loyal. Each look, word, and touch with Eva was out of this world. He had no idea that depth of feeling and sparks existed in romantic relationships from simple touches. What would kissing her feel like?

He let out a heavy sigh, pushing that dream from his mind. What a mess. How to explain to Eva? He couldn't. He'd sound like a wishy-washy loser who'd held onto the girl waiting for him back home for too long—twelve years too long, truth be told. Now he was willing to make a change because he'd met a famous and beautiful actress. Eva wouldn't think he was much of a man and surely wouldn't believe she was special to him. If only he could show Eva how drawn he was to her, and that it had nothing to do with her stardom.

Walking out of the suite, his gaze locked on hers as she stood on the stairs, still backed against the railing and clinging to it.

"All clear," he said, forcing a smile. "I'll hurry down to my room and shower quick so I don't stink."

"You don't," she said softly.

"That's good news." He stepped back and gestured into the master suite. "I'll just need a few minutes."

She nodded, ascended the stairs, and breezed past him. She didn't get close enough to brush him, didn't smile or say anything.

Heading quickly down to the bedroom he was using, he stripped out of his running clothes, took the quickest shower of record, dressed, and was back to the main level before she came down from the master.

Had she really wanted to kiss him? Was it only a kiss of gratitude she'd wanted? Had she felt a bond between them, or was that all in his head?

Her soft footsteps treaded along the wide balcony upstairs and then she appeared. The oxygen sucked out of the room and Miles's chest somehow expanded at the same time. He could not breathe and would pass out if this kept going.

Was it possible she was more beautiful than ten minutes ago? Maybe it was because he'd been reminded by the near kiss that she was out of his reach, even if she was interested.

Once again, he wanted to kick himself. He could've kissed his dream woman, but his sense of honor wouldn't allow it. How soon could he fly home, make a clean break with Lily, figure out how to help Lily as a friend, and then fly back to Eva? He was certain he'd missed his one chance with Eva. He'd turned her down and missed kissing her when she'd been coming on to him strong. She'd been grateful for his protection and looked at him like a hero. It had been a once in a lifetime opportunity and now it was gone.

She yanked her gaze away and walked down the stairs. He noticed she focused on his nose, not his eyes or his mouth.

Maybe he should excuse himself, call Lily and end things,

then rush back to Eva. He'd gather her in his arms, tell her he was an idiot and there was no girl back home, and then he would kiss her until Aiden sorted out the mess she was in.

The connection between him and Eva had him edging closer. "Eva," he murmured. She met his gaze and everything settled. Of course Eva was the right one for him. Of course Lily would understand when he ended a thirteen-year relationship with a quick phone call.

No, he mentally yelled at himself. That was chicken crap. He was a Navy SEAL, a gentleman cowboy, a Christian, and a Coleville. His dad and heaven above wouldn't accept him treating Lily like that. He wouldn't accept it. She was an incredible lady and deserved better. It was on him that he hadn't ended things six months ago.

Because of his duty to Lily, Eva would be back to her acting world before he was free to explain fully and pursue her. Eva was as far out of his reach now as she had been when she didn't know him from Adam.

He stepped back and focused out the windows. The pool glowed blue, and a container ship was crawling past in the distance.

"Anything from Aiden?" she asked, her voice chipper, fake, not the real Eva he kept kidding himself he knew so well.

"Not yet." He steeled himself to look at her and forced a smile to match hers. "He'll be thorough and get the answers you need so we can keep you safe." It wouldn't be him keeping her safe. Would it? Could he volunteer? He wasn't one of Aiden's bodyguards, and he only had four days until he had to be back on base.

"That'll be great. Thanks again for being here for me, rescuing me."

"Happy to do it."

This stilted conversation hurt.

"Are you hungry or thirsty?" he asked.

"No thank you."

He drummed his fingers on the counter. What would they do until Aiden called? How long could it take to expose a dirty FBI agent? He almost smiled at that. It could take days or weeks, maybe months. Just him and Eva. Stuck in Aiden's house until they got some answers. And he couldn't pursue her or even talk to her normally.

"How long have you been in the Navy?" she asked.

"Twelve years." He appreciated her trying to converse. "I left home right after high school graduation. I always wanted to be a SEAL."

"And now you're a lieutenant with your SEAL unit?" She smiled. "Impressive."

"Thank you. Not as impressive as everything you've accomplished in ten years." Her high school drama teacher had a connection in Hollywood and Eva had landed a role in a movie that took off right out of high school. Her career had launched quickly and now she was an A-lister.

She arched her eyebrows and settled onto a padded barstool. He pulled one out and sat down as well.

"Is it lame of me to admit that I hate that you know everything about me and I know nothing about you?" She bit at her lip.

Miles was grateful she wanted to know anything about him. The 'girl back home' comment seemed to linger between them.

"I don't know everything about you," he said.

"Oh really? So you don't follow me on social media, don't watch my movies and interviews, didn't think it would be cool to meet and flirt with the famous Eva Chevron?" She didn't sound confrontational, more disappointed.

Miles couldn't lie to her, and that was a huge disadvantage right now.

"You're right." He spread his hands and grimaced at the vindicated and disappointed look in her dark eyes. "I was enamored with you, like most single men over thirteen, but I was enamored because I saw clips of you helping an older gentleman across the street, bending down and chatting with the children your co-workers ignored, standing by an actress friend when others defamed her, and you have to admit it's incredible that you have an original number ninety-nine Wayne Gretzky King's jersey."

She actually smiled at that.

Maybe he should've stopped, but his tongue rattled on. "After meeting you, I'm even more impressed with how bravely you've handled this crazy night and how genuine and intriguing you are." He took a breath, wishing he could say how her touch lit him up, how he imagined they had a unique and incredible bond. It was only fair that she knew. "Eva, the real you is a million times more impressive than your actress persona. I was enamored with you before. Now I'm mesmerized."

"Thank you, Miles." Her words were sincere. At least she'd accepted the compliment.

Their gazes met and held. Miles forgot his obligation to his SEAL unit, his family, Lily, his honor. Nothing mattered at this moment but Eva. She was destined to become the most important part of his life, and in her deep-brown eyes he could read that she felt the same way.

She moistened her lips, and he leaned in before he could stop himself.

His phone buzzed in his pocket. He pushed out a heavy breath, straightened, and ripped out his phone. It was a needed but unwelcome interruption.

"Yeah," he barked into the phone without meaning to.

"Sorry to interrupt," Aiden chirped, "but we have loads of bad news for our favorite actress."

"That doesn't sound good." He turned to Eva. She stood from the barstool, her eyes wary. He pushed the speaker button. "Eva's right here."

"Eva." Aiden's cultured voice sounded heavy. "We don't have any definite answers for you, but we have discovered that throughout his FBI career Ryken Henderson has been reprimanded for withholding evidence, prosecuted for taking a bribe, though that charge didn't stick, and passed over for promotions. His file is thick, and not because of successful cases. The eeriest thing is he's not even a field agent any longer. He's been relegated to research and he definitely isn't assigned to your case. In fact, no one is."

"So he shouldn't even have contacted me?" Eva asked.

"Correct. He must've seen the concerns with Jorge in a police report and gotten the idea to use it to get close to you. From what we can gather, he told the police he was taking over and nobody even questioned him or checked with his superiors."

Eva's throat bobbed. "Dang."

"The good news is we can blow the whistle on Ryken and Eva can go back to her life," Miles said.

The look she gave him was chilly. Did she not want to go back to her life?

"I don't believe that is possible," Aiden said.

"Why not?" Eva asked.

"When my people were digging on information about Jorge, Ryken, and you, they found some very concerning bounties on the dark web."

"Bounties? For what?" Eva asked.

Miles instinctively edged closer to Eva. He wasn't making a move; he was trying to support her.

"There were seven different requests from a variety of shadow corporations," Aiden said. "Every one had at least a million dollar payment attached to it. Every one was centered around kidnapping Eva Chevron."

Eva's face blanched. She stepped back, to sit on the barstool possibly, but she missed and stumbled.

Miles caught her around the waist and hauled her against his chest. He held her close and whispered, "It's all right. I'm here. I've got you."

Her deep-brown eyes focused on him, and he knew he'd do anything for her.

"I apologize, Eva," Aiden said on the phone. "I know this is shocking."

"Horrifying," she admitted, leaning into Miles.

"I'm sorry." Aiden's voice was sincere. Though he dealt with issues like this, or worse, multiple times a day, he wasn't the type to make light of someone's fears or suffering.

"Do you think I've had requests on the dark web before?" Eva asked.

"Yes, you have," Aiden said calmly.

"Excuse me?" Eva straightened and looked at Miles with wide eyes.

"My tech people, Sutton Smith's team, and various government agencies keep their eyes out for requests like these and will pass the information on to law enforcement, and to the target if necessary. But they have to honestly evaluate the risk versus the person's emotional well-being. Do you want to live your life fearing you're a target, or do you recognize that you are a public figure and may have depraved fans or people looking to make money from you or your fame? Most celebrities have decent security, are prepared for such things, and most hits on the dark web don't get fulfilled."

"But you think whoever is after me will get their request fulfilled?"

"I don't like the coincidence of you being attacked, an FBI agent who isn't on the up and up trying to gain your trust, Jorge sending you all these notes, and most disturbing of all, seven separate requests, all with high-dollar figures appearing within the hour. There have been no police reports of you being attacked tonight and your house is clean, locked up, no lights on, no sign of the attacker or the struggle on the patio. It's disturbing. If I rated clients in danger from one to ten, your risk profile would be eight point two, and that is only because Lieutenant Miles Coleville is standing next to you. Without Miles, your chances of making it through the night without being abducted are at about zero point four."

Miles appreciated the endorsement, but not the fear in Eva's eyes. Did Aiden need to come on so strong? Maybe he'd learned he had to, or people in danger wouldn't listen and unwittingly put themselves in more danger. Miles had experienced that in foreign countries on diplomatic missions.

Eva's mouth opened, but nothing came out. She stepped away from Miles and balled her hands into fists. "What am I supposed to do? Hire your company?" She looked from Miles to the phone. "How do I know you didn't set this all up to make money off me or brag about your latest celebrity security detail?"

It was similar to when she'd been reluctant to step into Aiden's house, but much more confrontational. She was scared and defensive. Miles didn't blame her. He didn't fear much, but seven separate million-dollar hits on the dark web? That would be unsettling to anyone.

"I feel my reputation can speak for itself." Aiden didn't sound offended at all. Probably because he recognized what Miles could see. Eva was terrified and maybe in shock. "I pray you will listen to me, Eva, and disappear until my people can research, track down leads, and get to the bottom of these requests. We'll figure out what Jorge Augilar and Ryken Henderson are all about."

"Disappear?" She leaned against the counter. "How can I just disappear? I have scenes to finish. I was supposed to go see my family."

"We can work out a plan to keep you safe, Eva, and eliminate the threats, but you're going to have to trust me."

A thick silence fell, and Eva worried her lip. Miles didn't know how to help. He had to get back to base, back to his men in four days.

As he studied Eva, he stewed about what he could do to help, if anything.

"You're Aiden Porter," Eva finally said. "I know you're trustworthy and I pray you'll forgive me for lashing out, but this is huge and scary and it's my life being flipped upside down."

"I understand that, Eva." Aiden's voice was soft. "I'm only trying to keep you safe and take out the threats without any risk to you. This is what I do, and I'm very, very good at it. In fact, I'm an expert."

Miles almost smiled at that. Aiden would never be called humble, but he was a trustworthy and successful security expert.

"I know you are," Eva said. "I've heard the chatter."

"Well, then ..." Aiden's voice had a hint of a tease in it now. "Miles? Are you ready to be temporarily employed by Porter Enterprises?"

"Um ... what?" Miles was a step behind.

"You've already gained her trust. You're right there. And to be completely honest, though I'll deny this if either of you have loose lips, my operatives are spread thin with Benjamin Oliver still on the loose and the need to protect many people from his deviousness and retaliations until I can rip him out of whatever hole he's hiding in."

Miles could imagine Aiden and Quaid were both busy protecting innocent victims Benjamin might target and hunting the man down. A defensive and offensive game with far too many innocents at risk and pitted against one of the most brilliant criminals any of them had dealt with.

"I will put my best people on solving Eva's dilemma," Aiden continued. "Shouldn't take long. I've got the connections to get you leave from your unit and I believe you know the place to keep a famed beauty safe for an unspecified amount of time."

Miles wanted to help and be there for Eva. He hoped it was for unselfish reasons, but he couldn't deny he'd like the chance to get to know her. If he could take her to Coleville, Montana, be near his family, and maybe have the long overdue conversation with Lily, he would be saying loads of prayers of gratitude.

"Aiden," he began, focused on Eva to see how she was taking all of this. "If you wanted to work your magic for a temporary leave from my unit, I could stay by Eva's side and take her to the ranch while your people research and eliminate the threats."

"What a brilliant idea. I thought you'd never offer," Aiden said, all cheery and smart-alecky. "Done from my end. Eva? Are you comfortable with Miles as your primary bodyguard? He will take you to a secure location. To a family of tough cowboys who protected Jacqueline Oliver for over a year without even a hint of a lead getting to her."

"That is impressive." Eva was still worrying her lip, but her shoulders weren't bunched as tightly around her ears. "What family is that?"

"Mine," Miles said, offering her a smile.

She didn't return it.

CHAPTER *Six*

EVA STARED AT MILES. What was she supposed to say? She'd never been more interested in a man, and he had a girlfriend. Why did he want to protect her, take her to his family's secure ranch, take leave from his unit to be there for her? Simply because she was famous, or he was just that honorable of a man? It didn't add up in her head that he had a girlfriend or 'girl back home', whatever that meant. Had that been an excuse so he wouldn't have to kiss Eva?

She was going insane worrying about Miles's girlfriend and his intentions toward her, and she should be worried about Ryken, Jorge, and the sadistic people who were offering all this money on the dark web to kidnap her.

But she did trust Miles. He'd rescued her tonight and proven he could keep her safe. She knew he was a good guy, an impressive warrior, and he would be there for her. She was simply annoyed about this faceless girl and wondering how she'd keep a distance from Miles when he felt like the man she'd longed for all her life. Being around him made her question why she'd ever dated a pompous snake like Lake. Miles was the complete and ideal man for her. His touch was like a fairy tale.

And he had a girl back home. The plan was to go to his home. What would that mean? Maybe his intentions were all focused on that girl. Aiden would get him leave and Miles could go see his lady. Ugh.

"Are you comfortable with this arrangement, Eva?" Aiden asked.

"Yes," she said before she could chicken out. She didn't have a better option. She doubted there was a better option out there. Aiden Porter's talented team would track down and take out the bad guys and she'd get to stay close to the handsome Navy SEAL lieutenant who made her feel safe. Now to keep her head 'screwed on straight' as her dad would say and not make the moves on Miles.

"You won't regret it. Miles is over-qualified, and he'll keep you safe. Paul, my pilot, and Autumn, one of my top operatives, will be there soon. Paul will escort you to Montana and then return to California and focus on this job. Autumn will get ahold of your friends and family, Eva, and spread the word you have a vicious flu bug and they shouldn't visit. She'll hunker down at your beach home. She's very good at impersonation."

"Won't that put her in danger?" Eva asked.

"She loves danger." Aiden chuckled, and Miles smiled. "We'll see who we can flush out. See who comes to visit and risks getting sick. Autumn will bring some extra clothes and toiletries for you to take with you. I'm sure Mama Millie will have plenty waiting for you as well. Prepare to be smothered, I mean nurtured, by the best in the industry." Aiden chuckled.

Miles laughed too, rubbing at his chin. "My mama's incredible."

"I bet you'll be happy to get home," she said.

"For sure. It's been too long."

"For the family?" She arched an eyebrow.

Miles's gaze was probing, just like her words. She shouldn't be so transparent.

"All right, you two," Aiden said. "I need to sign off. Be in touch soon."

He was gone.

Miles pocketed his phone and glanced at her. "Are you all right?"

She hugged herself. "My life's being uprooted and I'm in demand on the dark web. All right is a bit of a stretch."

He smiled, taking no offense. "Adds up. Are you all right with me being your bodyguard?"

"Shouldn't I be?" She studied him. What was he trying to say?

He looked away for a moment. "I am qualified."

Eva couldn't get over how humble he was. Qualified? He was over-qualified; Aiden had said as much. Even going further and saying earlier that he'd trust his wife Chalisa to Miles's care and Miles was the only reason she'd survive the night.

"You didn't have much of a choice," Miles pointed out.

"I don't have much choice in any of this, but I appreciate you being willing to watch out for me. I'm sure your men will be missing you."

"Nah. They'll be relieved to not have me barking at them." He smiled at that, and she returned it.

One of the garage door motors sounded. Eva jumped and hurried behind Miles.

"It's all right," he assured her, putting one hand on her arm and pulling his gun out with the other. "It'll be Paul and Autumn."

"If it's all right, why are you grabbing your gun?"

"Because you can never be too careful." He ushered her back behind the wide kitchen counter, placing himself directly in front of her. He smelled like an alluring mix of bergamot and pineapple. It distracted her from her fears.

"Duck if I say duck," he told her, blocking her view of whoever might be coming in from the garage entrance.

Eva's heart beat high and fast. The Tylenol had calmed her headache, but the fear ratcheted up the throbbing in her skull again.

The door into the laundry room opened and closed. Heels clicked on the tile and a sultry female voice said, "Well hello there, Lieutenant Coleville. You do know how to greet a lady."

"Autumn." Miles visibly relaxed and lowered his gun. He turned and brought Eva level with him. "It's all right," he told her. "This is the woman Aiden told you about."

"Oh. It's nice to meet you." Eva stared at the exquisitely beautiful brunette. Her heels made her a few inches taller than Eva in her bare feet. There was something captivating about her —a mix of the confidence that she could kick anyone's behind, the defined muscles in her arms and legs that backed up her kicking their behind, and the golden eyes that appeared deceptively sweet. Eva had never seen golden eyes before. Were they real?

"You as well, Eva Chevron." Autumn's face softened in a genuine smile. "I am a huge fan. When you played Charli in *Protecting the Heiress* and took down the hunky Fitz ... ahh, happy sigh. You made women warriors the world over cheer. Forgive me. I'm gushing, and I never gush."

"No. I ... Thank you." Eva never knew quite how to respond to a gushing fan. How to be appreciative and humble? "I believe that you're not a gusher."

Autumn winked. "Come now. Paul is waiting in the garage for us."

"Let me grab my bag from the basement," Miles said.

"Hurry," Autumn urged.

"I will." Miles smiled and shook his head. He put the gun in the back of his waistband and pumped down the stairs.

"Whew. That man is a fine one." Autumn gave an exaggerated grimace. "You did not hear that from me. Professional conduct is encouraged in my industry." She winked and grinned as if she took nothing seriously.

"My lips are sealed." Eva liked this warrior woman. She had friends in Hollywood, but it was rare to meet someone who said whatever they thought and felt so genuine. "How did you become a woman warrior? That is fabulous."

"Very long story." Autumn suddenly looked closed off. "But you and Miles?"

"No." Eva shook her head. "He rescued me tonight. I'd never met him until an hour ago."

Autumn lifted her eyebrows. "Hmm. There is a load of chemistry between you. Sizzling."

"Professional conduct is encouraged?" Eva teased. "Do you get in trouble for being too blunt?"

Autumn laughed loudly at that. "I do not. In our flipped every direction world, which of my tough, honorable male counterparts would dare call out a female bodyguard? Even if they realize I'm all tease and I would never take advantage of my power. I can make the toughest guy out there blush and stammer. I've got them all exactly where I want them. Drooling over me, sometimes rising to my bait and teasing with me, but never daring to do a darn thing about it. Ah, there's our favorite humble, gorgeous, and accomplished lieutenant." Autumn clapped her hands together. "Chop chop."

Miles appeared at the top of the stairs an instant after Autumn clapped. Eva wasn't certain how Autumn had even heard him coming. Sixth sense? Miles's gaze zoned in on Eva and her stomach hopped. Every descriptor Autumn had thrown out there was true as well as the chemistry between them. But she wasn't about to do anything about it. 'Never daring to do a darn thing about it' in Autumn's words. He had a girl back home, and they were going to his home, apparently.

Autumn dropped her voice and whispered to Eva, "Sizzling." Her golden eyes sparkled, and it was obvious she saw straight through Eva. She turned and strode back out the garage entrance.

"What was that all about?" Miles asked as he reached Eva, a duffel bag in one hand. They walked much more slowly to the garage.

"She's a whirlwind," Eva said. "I like her."

"From what I understand, everyone does, but she keeps them on their toes."

"It sounds like it," Eva agreed.

They walked through the laundry room. Miles held the door for her, and they entered the darkened garage. Lights lit up the interior of a silver Lexus SUV. A handsome dark-haired man waited in the driver's seat, and Autumn had settled in the front passenger seat. Miles opened the rear door for Eva. She slid in.

He shut it and came around to the other side, stowing his bag behind him in the third row before climbing in.

"Eva Chevron, meet retired Air Force Reconnaissance Pilot Lieutenant Paul Braven," Autumn said.

"I'm honored, Miss Chevron," Paul said, pushing a button to open the garage door again.

"Nice to meet you. Please call me Eva. That is quite the title, Lieutenant Braven."

"Well, Paul is quite the man," Autumn said, giving him an appreciative look. "Please call him Paul. This pilot is a stud every girl on earth is gone over."

Miles chuckled even as Paul's neck darkened. He shook his head and focused on backing out of the garage and turning the car around. As he waited for the front gate to slide open, he said, "Autumn's life quest is to keep all the male operatives on their toes and second-guessing every word they say. Especially if she can make us feel awkward around the likes of Eva Chevron."

"I think you've got the awkwardness around Eva down pat all by yourself." Autumn grinned and patted his arm to add insult to injury.

Eva wanted to protest and ease Paul's discomfort, but Autumn continued, "But I do thrive on teasing you. And when I find a man who can dish it back and beat me in a sparring match, I will look up at him from the flat of my back and proclaim my love, finished with my life's quest and ready to settle down and make beautiful babies."

Eva barked out a laugh, and they all smiled at her.

"I like you, Eva Chevron," Autumn proclaimed.

"The feeling is mutual," Eva said.

"I love your laugh," Miles said.

The oxygen popped audibly from Eva's lungs. How was she

supposed to respond to that? He couldn't go loving her laugh. He had a girl.

He turned forward. "We should introduce Autumn to Easton," he said to Paul.

"Oh, definitely," Paul said. "Just another reason why we love the Coleville family."

"Remind me," Autumn said.

"The Coleville cowboys have not signed an employment contract with Aiden that specifies at the top of the first page, right after swearing to devote our lives to protecting the innocent and eradicating evil ... 'Under no circumstances are male operatives allowed to dish it back to Autumn or beat her at sparring and knock her onto her back.'"

"Ah, very funny. You've never *let* me win."

"I signed the contract, now didn't I?"

Eva smiled at their banter, feeling much more relaxed. "Who is Easton?"

"Yes, who is this specimen of a man who can keep up with my wit and fighting skills?"

"My brother," Miles said. "A famous bull rider and ultra-tough and charming cowboy who puts your flirtations to shame, Autumn."

"You had me at your brother." Autumn grinned even as Eva's gut tightened. Why did the woman claim Eva and Miles had sparks between them, and then flirt with him nonstop? "Does he look like you, Lieutenant Coleville?"

"Remarkably. The two years younger and much more handsome and charming version," Miles said. He glanced over at Eva. She wanted to tell him no one was more handsome or charming than him, but he had a girl back home. Why had she agreed to go to his ranch? Would she meet this lucky woman? It was exhilarating and at the same time difficult to be around him, knowing she could never be with him.

"Sign me up," Autumn said. "Though truth be told, I'd take the original." She gave Miles a wink and Eva a sly smile. "If the two of you didn't have sparks crackling between you."

Eva froze. An awkward tension filled the backseat—no sparks crackling like Autumn had said.

"Ah, now I've gone and made it awkward, haven't I?" Autumn tsked and looked to Paul. "Get us to the airport quick so I can send you all on your awkward way. Unfortunately, I must stay here and pretend to be Eva, sick in bed. I don't have to smell like vomit or cold-induced sweats to complete the picture, do I? I certainly hope some idiot who dared put a dark web bounty on my friend Eva's head comes to visit." She lifted her phone. "If not, I'll have plenty to keep me busy, Googling my future boyfriend's bull riding videos."

"Easton is going to devour this attention," Miles said. "Forget I said anything."

"Ah, no. Too late now. You've made my week. Fresh blood." She held up a video of a bull rider flying around like a cowboy rag doll on a huge bull's back.

Eva sucked in a breath. She'd watched bull riding at rodeos growing up, but it had been a while. She'd forgotten how vicious the event was.

"Don't worry." Miles put his hand over hers where it rested on the seat. The warm pressure of his hand lit a fire within her.

"Look at that," Autumn exclaimed.

Eva yanked her hand back, face flaring red, but Autumn wasn't looking at or exclaiming over them touching hands.

"He rode out the full eight seconds with style. What a man."

Eva could see the cowboy, Easton Coleville apparently, leap

clear of the bull, who immediately spun and zeroed in on him. The bullfighters distracted the massive brute animal, and a horse with a cowboy on his back flew to Easton's side. Easton swung up behind the horseman and waved to the cheering crowd.

"Future boyfriend for certain," Autumn said. "Put in a good word for me, Miles."

Miles chuckled. "Don't worry, I will."

"Tell Easton not to hold his breath," Paul teased. "Autumn will never let her guard down for any man."

"Ah, now." Autumn patted his hand on the steering wheel. "I am proud of you for taking your shot. Really, I am. It's not you, it's me." She fluttered her lashes.

Eva felt bad for Paul, but he laughed as loud as she'd heard him laugh. "Ah, Autumn. If any of us thought we had a shot, we might take it. And it is definitely *you* not me. I'm one of the few people in our industry who doesn't have relationship issues."

Autumn joined him in his laughter. "That's why you're thirty-five and still single."

"Just waiting for you."

"Patience is such a sweet characteristic, but it will never win this lady's heart." She put a hand dramatically over her heart and one over her eyes.

Eva and Miles joined in their laughter as they kept bantering. She was grateful they'd moved on from the tension of Autumn teasing her and Miles about sparks, but she wished she hadn't pulled her hand away. She could be enjoying the show in the front seat with Miles's hand cupping hers.

CHAPTER Seven

MILES WAS RELIEVED to say goodbye to Autumn at Aiden's private hangar and climb aboard a quiet Cessna Citation with Paul and Eva. Autumn was hilarious, but she was a bit much to take. He did appreciate her pushing Eva at him though. His charming and overconfident younger brother Easton would definitely meet his match if they ever met in person.

Paul made certain they were settled in and then went up front to do preflight checks. The door to the plane beeped and automatically swung out and down.

Miles leaped in front of Eva's seat, whipping his Sig out. Eva's breathing increased.

"I'm here," he murmured. "Don't worry."

Paul flung open the cockpit door, his pistol out as well. He would've received notification the door had opened. Only someone with the right remote could open it. It was most likely Autumn, but a criminal could have overpowered her, no matter how tough she talked or how tough she was.

"Don't get trigger-happy on me," Autumn called out, sashaying up the steps with a small carry-on in her hand. "I forgot the clothes and goodies for my new best friend."

Miles and Paul both lowered their sidearms. Eva stood and eased around next to Miles. His pulse took off as her arm brushed against his. It was an accidental touch, but every touch with her was unique and enticing. He passed his free hand over his face.

"Autumn." Paul pushed out a heavy breath. "Somebody is going to shoot you one of these days, always trying to shock and tease us all."

"Nah. My boys are too exceptionally trained and love me far too much."

"We do love you," Paul admitted. "Like the annoying little sister who never grew up."

Autumn blew him a kiss.

"Thank you," Eva said, taking the suitcase from her.

"You got it, girlie. Now you go enjoy and don't worry about a thing. Miles will take good care of his beautiful actress, that's for sure."

"I'm not his," Eva murmured, not looking at him.

Miles feared he'd never get the chance to make her his.

"You think sparks like yours happen every day?" Autumn tsked. "Not in my lifetime."

"Please." Eva lowered her voice and leaned into Autumn's ear. "He has a girl," she said quietly, but it still carried to Miles.

Autumn's eyes widened and her gaze flew to Miles. Her dark eyes were full of challenge and annoyance. "That's no never mind of yours. You're Eva Chevron. No girl can compete with you."

Miles looked away. He couldn't handle the censure in

Autumn's eyes at having never heard about a girlfriend or the fact that he was hurting Eva. Even worse was the defeated posture he'd never seen Eva Chevron display.

"That is hardly the point," Eva said, straightening her shoulders, her voice as cool as it had been since he'd met her. "Thank you, Autumn. Stay safe. I hope to see you again."

"You as well. We'd be the best of girlie friends. Ta-ta."

Autumn and Eva shared a quick embrace and then Autumn glared at him. "Miles. Figure your junk out." She marched off the plane. The door shut behind her.

Eva walked over and settled into a recliner. Miles sat next to her. He wished he had any idea what to say. Autumn kept making things more awkward for him. Then he realized … he was taking Eva to the ranch. Easton and Walker would be worse than teenage boys around her, either hoping to get her attention for themselves or trying to push her to Miles. Never mind that the 'billboard of manly cowboy heroism' Sheriff Clint Coleville would be around as well. Lily had dropped that line on him. Twice. He'd told her to go after Clint once. She said she'd never dare. Miles knew he was handsome, tough, and brave, but nobody could compete with Clint.

The plane taxied out of the massive hangar door. He loved his brothers and would never try to compete with them for women. Not that he'd ever gone after anyone but Lily. He knew nothing about the dating game. And he thought he could have a chance with the most incredible woman created? What a joke. Instead of laughing, he blew out a heavy breath.

Eva glanced sharply at him.

"Sorry," he said.

"For?" She lifted a delicate eyebrow.

"Autumn. She's a lot to take sometimes."

"I liked *her*. I liked her a lot."

What was with the emphasis? "Only her?" Miles challenged when he should be brainstorming how to counteract the 'girl back home' comment he never should've made. He could've flown home, flirted with and grown closer to Eva the entire time, found a break to go visit Lily, and then made his play for Eva.

No, he couldn't. Not if he wanted to sleep at night.

"You don't meet a lot of genuinely honest people who are true to their character like Autumn and seem to really enjoy themselves. Not in Hollywood, at least."

"Hmm." Was there something underlying there, and why was he suddenly reading something into her words? He was a man. He didn't stress over every word spoken. "Well, luckily you're headed to Coleville, Montana, ma'am. The cowboys there are as genuine as the day is long."

That was a stupid line. Was he trying to push her on his brothers?

She studied him, as if reading something into his words. The plane stopped momentarily, and he knew Paul would be getting clearance to take off.

"I like genuine," she said.

Did she think he hadn't been genuine with her? If he'd wanted to lie, he sure wouldn't have told her about Lily. Not that he'd shared much. He felt like he'd shared just enough to incriminate himself. What explanation could he attempt to give her that wouldn't make it worse? He was in a lose-lose situation —finding the woman of his dreams while still halfway committed to the woman who'd waited years for him.

"How many brothers do you have?" she asked.

"Five brothers, six counting me."

"Oh my. Your poor mother."

He laughed. "She loves it. Her boys are the highlight of her life. Of course she nags us all about getting married and making beautiful grandbabies."

Her eyes widened. "Tell me about your brothers, please. Start at the top."

When Miles agreed to protect her and take her home, he'd been focused on keeping Eva safe and, in the back of his mind, finding a chance to talk to Lily and be free to pursue Eva. He hadn't stopped to think about his lineup of handsome, tough, and impressive brothers surrounding her. And none of them had a 'girl' currently. Shoot.

"Clint's the oldest," he began. "The sheriff of our county."

"Impressive."

"He is," he admitted.

The plane picked up speed, racing along the runway.

"How old is Clint?"

"Thirty-two."

"Married?"

"No, ma'am. A lady broke his heart six months ago, two weeks before their wedding day."

"That's awful."

"It was." He despised Sheryl Dracon. An angelic face and a dragon's heart. Sheryl had two-timed Clint and their friend and neighbor Cade Miller. Cade was happily married to the infamous Jacqueline Oliver now. The two of them were in hiding from her at-large criminal of a father.

"I'm next in line."

She only nodded. No follow-up questions.

The plane got up to speed and lifted off, soaring quickly up into the night air. The wheels thumped back into the undercarriage.

"Then the twins, Easton and Walker. They're twenty-eight. Easton is a bull rider as you saw, and Walker is the roper. He prefers steer roping, but it's only recognized in ten states, so he mostly does tie-down roping."

"It's recognized in Wyoming," she said.

"It is."

"You forget I'm from a ranch too."

"I couldn't forget anything about you, Eva," he said softly.

She didn't roll her eyes, but he sensed she wanted to. He knew more about her than she wanted him to. He'd really messed things up not kissing her earlier, but what could he do to rectify such a mistake? Nothing until he spoke with Lily.

"That's four. Who's next?"

"Rhett. He's twenty-six, owns his own construction company and builds custom vacation homes and cabins near Kalispell."

"Nice."

"Houston's the baby. Twenty-four, he's the brilliant one among us. Undergrad done in two years instead of four. Now he's in the middle of his residency in family practice in Omaha. Mama originally prayed for him to be a brain surgeon, but now she's grateful he chose family practice and praying he'll move home and take over Doc's practice. Doc is a good-old boy and retirement is definitely on his radar."

"And your parents own the ranch where I'll supposedly be safe?"

"You'll be safe. We take our safety seriously, and my brothers and the ranch hands are almost as tough as I am." He gave her what he hoped was a confident smile. He never bragged about himself, and it felt awkward.

"I look forward to meeting them."

That stirred something uncomfortable in his gut. His brothers were handsome, devastatingly so. Or so he'd heard. Easton was a flirt to the tenth degree. Walker had the slow cowboy grin and kind heart women went nuts over. Clint was the tough, reserved Sheriff, and women vied to break through his shell. Rhett was the successful contractor, and everybody knew about women and tool belts. Houston ... the doctor thing was too appealing to even think about competing with.

He highly doubted they'd see Houston or Rhett. Still, Miles was in trouble when the rest of them met Eva Chevron. A lot of trouble.

"I'm going to try to rest," Eva said. "Tonight has felt longer than the preacher's sermon on patience."

He smiled. "I'm sure it has."

She pushed the button that reclined the chair and closed her eyes. Miles found the remote that dimmed the lights in the cabin.

"Thank you," she murmured, not opening her eyes.

"Sure." Miles should try to rest too. He'd be on duty round the clock when they got to the ranch.

Instead, he schemed how he could keep her away from his brothers. Her safety had to come first, and his brothers were impressive and well-trained, but so were the ranch hands. He'd meet with his dad as soon as they got there, see which ranch hands were married and could help him out. Then he'd keep Eva in his cabin, keep her all to himself. They couldn't risk her beautiful and famous face being recognized if someone happened to visit the ranch.

He slumped in his seat, knowing his dad would blow holes in these arguments. Eva was safest in the main house, and nobody came through their gates without the front gate guard letting them in and the guard monitoring the security cameras and sensors knowing they had a guest and relaying everything about the guest. They could easily hide Eva if someone came to visit. This definitely wasn't their first rodeo of security details. Jacey Oliver's year of hiding at their ranch was bragging rights they'd never tell anyone about.

If only he could officially break up with Lily and make his own play for Eva. He had the connection with her, had rescued her, knew how brave and kind she was. If he could tell her all the reasons they were perfect together, maybe his brothers wouldn't stand a chance.

Then again, they might beat him out even if he was playing with a full deck. Being a Coleville brother was both a blessing and a curse.

CHAPTER Eight

EVA COULD FEEL Miles studying her. She resolutely kept her eyes shut, proud of her acting skills with her hatred of inactivity. She must've drifted off, because she woke to the plane landing. It was smooth. Paul, the Air Force too-long title guy who liked to tease Autumn, was a great pilot.

She felt groggy and awful. Like a cow who'd been driven on the range all night long, then branded with a hot, burning iron before breakfast.

"What time is it?" she asked, her voice scratchy, keeping her eyes closed. Thankfully, the cabin lights were still dim.

"Almost one in the morning," Miles said. "Here." He pressed a cold plastic bottle into her hands. "How's your head?"

"Thank you. It's still attached, unfortunately."

He chuckled softly.

She blinked her eyes open and peered at his face in the dim light. Why did he have to be so appealing and so taken? She twisted off the lid and took a long drink, blinking quickly. "Do I have time to use the restroom?"

"Of course." He pointed at a door in the back of the plane as they taxied to a stop.

She took another drink of her water bottle and left it in the cup holder. Standing, she felt disoriented and dizzy.

Miles sprang to his feet and wrapped his arm around her waist, drawing her in to his solid, steady, warm, perfect, desirable, bergamot and pineapple, head-clouding, enticing side. Okay, she had to stop this. Where was Autumn or Tasha when she needed them? A girlfriend or sister would be such a help. There was too much stress surrounding tonight, and her longing for Miles was helping nothing.

She peered up into Miles's eyes. In the dim light, they were more of a smoky blue. How did he smell so enticingly manly? "Was I teetering like the town drunk?"

"I don't know. We don't have a town drunk in Coleville." He winked and grinned.

She laughed. "Ha ha. Only in Wyoming can anybody drink excessively."

He smiled. "You did look unsteady though. Which is why I … wrapped you up."

"Is that the only reason?" She could've bitten her own tongue in half.

His eyes darkened, and she thought he might show her the real reason he wrapped her up, but he only asked, "Are you all right?"

"Sure. Exhausted, overwhelmed, terrified, wishing I had my purse and phone and my bed and my life back."

"I'm sorry to take all those things from you. I will take care of you, Eva. Aiden and his people are incredible. They will fix all of this."

"Thank you."

She moistened her lips, and his gaze sharpened on her mouth. His arm around her made her feel like she was happily floating. Before she could even think about what she was doing, she wrapped her palms around his broad shoulders and was pulling herself up toward his enticing mouth.

The cockpit door opened, and Miles quickly turned her with his arm. "The bathroom is this way."

Awkward.

He walked her to the bathroom as if she were an old lady who'd lost her cane. Opening the door, he ushered her in. Automatic lights came on, and Eva shut the door—too firmly. She looked in the mirror. It was worse than she thought. Red-rimmed eyes, dark smudges underneath her eyes from mascara that hadn't stayed put, and no lip-stain left on her dry-looking lips. Oh, boy. She looked worse than a drowned rat.

What did it matter? Miles was taken. Had he leaned down, or had she only arched up? As she replayed the near-kiss in her mind, she realized with horror ... She had been the only one who'd made a move. The only willing participant. He also hadn't risen to her baiting him and asking if he had another reason for wrapping her up in his arms.

Ah, no. She pressed a hand to her forehead. Miles was acting as her bodyguard, wrapping an arm around her to steady her and saying he'd take care of her. She took every look, every touch, every kind word as if he wanted to kiss her.

Out of control. That's what she was. Desperate for love? Maybe Lake had destroyed her confidence just like her sister Tasha had feared. When she first went to Hollywood and had quick success, she'd dated a lot of actors, athletes, and influencers. She'd learned that they were looking for the 'next best thing'. For years she'd kept herself safe emotionally and physically, perfecting the art of being kind and fun but distant. Except for her mistake of trusting Lake. Her feelings toward Miles were strong, unexpected. In her mind, they had something unique, but that couldn't be true for him.

Somehow, she needed to keep her distance from her own bodyguard. That wouldn't work. She needed to channel some of Autumn's sass, then, and pray for strength.

Please help me not throw myself at Miles and be obsessed with him. Please bless that Aiden, Paul, and Autumn can fix the huge mess I'm in and I can return home.

It was interesting to note that she was obsessed with Miles. She'd had many, many men obsessed with her. Jorge Augilar had been the most terrifying, but she'd had stalking situations, notes, presents, flowers, men calling to her that she was meant to be their wife. Now she was the one obsessing over a too-appealing man. It was worse from this angle. At least she could gain some empathy for her male fans through the experience.

She used the bathroom quickly, washed her hands, splashed some water on her face, and rummaged through the cupboards. She found lip gloss, travel-size mascara, and vanilla-scented lotion. Ah, that was thoughtful. She hurriedly eradicated the black smudges, fixed her mascara, and put on the lip gloss and lotion. Bless whoever had left these on the plane. Most likely Chalisa Porter. Too late, she realized it was crossing boundaries to use someone's lip gloss and mascara. It was the country girl coming out in her.

"Sorry," she muttered to Chalisa.

At least she looked more like herself. She could face Miles

with her chin held high. She walked out and Miles was waiting for her. He smiled, holding the small suitcase.

"Paul just gave the all-clear to exit the aircraft. My brother's waiting."

"Which brother?"

"Clint."

"That was nice of the sheriff to come."

"I doubt Aiden gave him much choice." He smiled, but it was grim. "Let's get you home so you can rest."

She stared at him. Get you home? It wasn't her home. Was he feeling awkward taking her 'home' when he had a girl at home? Would she meet this lucky woman? She prayed not.

"Thanks."

Miles took her hand and escorted her off the plane. She wanted to take exception to that as he wasn't a free man and holding hands meant you were a couple in her mind, but she was too tired and confused to know where to start right now, what to think. She savored the feel of his large hand surrounding hers. He was her bodyguard and an honorable cowboy and Navy SEAL, not her future. She needed to repeat that a few hundred times.

They walked out into a cool summer night. She hadn't felt the fresh touch of a mountain summer's night since Wyoming. Ah. The dry air. The scent of sagebrush and pine. The sparkling stars filling the sky beyond the small airport's lights. It was familiar and beautiful, and maybe Montana was almost as good as Wyoming.

Miles walked her to a white four-door truck where a tall, fit cowboy waited. She could easily see the family resemblance in the strong jaw and blue eyes. Miles's brother wore boots, jeans, and a T-shirt. The outfit showcased his well-built frame without even trying to. He had a cowboy hat on even though it was nighttime and leaned casually against his truck with one boot crossed over the other as he talked to Paul. He wasn't posturing like most men in her world would. She doubted this guy knew what the word 'preen' meant. He was simply John Wayne reincarnated. This man fit the image of every cowgirl's dreams.

Not hers, though. She glanced up at Miles, then quickly away. She'd met the man of her dreams earlier tonight, and he was taken.

Miles's brother focused on her, straightened to full height, and tilted the tip of his cowboy hat down. "Ma'am."

Eva couldn't help but smile, especially when she noticed Miles's hand tightening around hers. "Hello." Her voice was shy, almost awe-struck. There was something about this guy. He engendered respect and wasn't someone you messed with. She doubted even Autumn would tease him. Well, Autumn probably would.

"Sheriff Clint Coleville. Pleased to meet you." He stuck out his hand. She tugged her hand free of Miles's to shake. Clint's handshake was firm, his hands calloused. He was a good-old boy to a T. She felt none of the sparks she felt from a simple brush of Miles's skin against hers.

Not that she'd admit to that.

"This is Eva Chevron," Miles said.

"I might be a hick sheriff from Montana, but I actually know who Eva Chevron is, little brother," Clint drawled. "Though she's even more beautiful in real life."

"Well, thank you. It's been a hot minute since I've been in the presence of a real-life cowboy sheriff. Not just an actor pretending to be one."

"Happy to oblige." He grinned and tipped his hat again.

There was no denying he was a handsome one with an appeal all his own. Sadly, he wasn't Miles. Sadly for her, nobody was, and Miles wasn't free.

"Good to see you, Clint." Miles and Clint clapped each other on the back. As they pulled back, Miles slugged his brother in the shoulder. Really hard.

"Not so little as you remember, maybe, big brother." Miles gave him a heartfelt smile as Clint shook his arm out. Eva hoped they wouldn't duke it out.

Paul chuckled.

"We'll see." Clint looked Miles over but thankfully didn't slug him back. The sheriff tilted his head to Eva. "We'd better get you home to Mama. She's been cooking, baking, and cleaning since we got the call from Aiden."

"She should be sleeping," Eva burst out.

"Try telling her that," Clint said, and he and Miles both laughed. It seemed to ease some of the tension.

"Thank you, Paul." Miles shook Paul's hand.

"Are you leaving?" Eva asked.

"Yes. Aiden's given me a break from flying all over the world to follow leads on your case and give Autumn a hard time." Paul grinned. "Very nice to have met you, Eva."

"Thank you."

Clint waved and walked around, opening the passenger side door. "Eva."

Miles grunted. He put a hand on her lower back and walked her around. Eva was instantly too warm. How would she stay impervious to him when her heart had fallen the instant he gave her that first smile when he ran the beach, and then been sealed his when he gallantly rescued her and she realized this humble yet gallant man's touch was magical to her?

Miles lifted her up into the large truck. His large hands encompassed her waist, and she was out of breath and everything but him forgotten.

He smiled at her. Instead of leaning in to kiss her, he released her and pressed the door to close it, but before it latched ...

"Navy SEAL bully," she heard Clint grunt at him, before he slugged him in the shoulder.

"Stop hitting on Eva," came a low growl.

Eva stared out her window. She feared they'd brawl right there, but they had a stare down that lasted a long, tense moment, then Clint smiled.

"You look good, bro. Lily will be happy to see you."

Lily. The girl was Lily. Her heart seemed to seize. Lily. It was a sweet and beautiful name. She would have to be a beautiful sweetheart to capture Miles Coleville's heart.

"You look good too. Sparring ring still in good condition?"

"Oh yeah."

"Perfect." Miles pumped his eyebrows. "Tomorrow?"

"Soon as I can get there."

Miles looked over at Eva and he must've realized the door wasn't shut as the interior truck light was still on. He gently shut her door and then loaded up directly behind her. Clint strutted around the front. It wasn't an actual strut because he wasn't trying to show off; he just oozed masculinity and didn't know how not to strut.

The ride home was quiet. Tense. What was going on with these two? Miles had spoken warmly about his brothers. Now they were slugging each other and setting up sparring times?

She must've drifted off again. She woke to the truck stopping and doors opening and closing. Blinking, she saw a large two-story lodge-style home with a welcoming front porch complete with flower boxes filled with brightly colored blooms and rocking chairs. Lights blazed in most of the downstairs windows. It had to be two a.m., but these people looked ready for an important guest. She supposed she *was* the important guest.

Her door opened and Miles offered her a hand and a smile. "I'll try to keep Mama's nurturing to a minimum tonight so you can get some rest in a bed."

"I've slept on the plane and in the truck. Maybe I don't need any more sleep."

"Maybe I'm the one who needs the sleep." He gave her a teasing smile.

She slid out of the truck and to her feet. Miles did not step back, and she found herself pressed against him. Her heart sped up and her thoughts scattered. Sparks lit the air between them.

Miles released her hand and gently cupped her hips with his large palms. Eva's hands instinctively rested on his chest. She savored the feel of firm muscle under her fingertips.

His blue eyes captivated her. "Eva," he whispered. "I—"

The front door banged open, and a woman cried out, "My boy!"

Miles stepped back and escorted her around the truck door, shutting it. "My mama," he said, ushering Eva forward as a lovely middle-aged brunette and a broad cowboy hurried to meet them. Two younger cowboys were behind them.

"Whoo-hoo!" one of the younger men whooped, swinging his cowboy hat around his head. "It really is Eva Chevron! Somebody punch me."

"Gladly," the other cowboy said and slugged him in the arm.

"Boys!" Miles's Mama harrumphed at them and rushed down the stairs.

Miles released Eva to pick his mama up off her feet and hug her tightly.

"Oh, love, you're home. I'm so happy!" His mama kissed his cheek. Miles set her down but kept her in the circle of his arm. "If you aren't the most handsome Navy SEAL on the planet, then I don't know how to bake."

Miles only laughed at that, but Eva wanted to shout her agreement.

"Mama, Papa, this is Eva Chevron." He sounded proud to introduce her, but she knew it was only her famous status, not that he was introducing her to his family because she meant something special to him.

Miles's dad shook her hand. "Nice to meet ya."

"It's a real honor, Eva," his mama said, hugging her. "We'll take right good care of you now. You're safe with my family watching over you. My boys are the bravest and toughest and smartest and most handsome men on the planet. But you've already noticed that, right?"

"Mama," Miles groaned, shaking his head.

"What? You don't brag about yourself near enough. You're a Navy SEAL hero and I can brag all I want. I'm the mama."

Eva couldn't hide her smile. Mama was great, and she was right that Miles didn't brag. It was one of his many incredible qualities.

"Why don't you brag more?" Mama insisted.

"Oh, Mama." Miles gave her another hug. "You brag enough for all of us."

Everyone cracked up at that. Mama put her hands on her hips. "Well, I never." She rolled her eyes. "Eva? You agree I have a right to brag."

"Yes, ma'am." What else was she supposed to say? Miles

gave her an appreciative look, his blue eyes lighting up the night for her.

"None of this ma'am stuff. You can call me Mama or Mama Millie. Whatever you like. Are you hungry, thirsty, simply exhausted?"

"Thank you, but I'm fine. You all shouldn't have stayed up waiting for me."

"Well, we had no choice, pretty lady," one of the younger men said. "It's not every day the most beautiful and incredible actress visits Coleville Ranch. I'm Easton, by the way, the perfect Navy SEAL's most handsome and charming brother who he conveniently forgot to introduce."

The other brother shoved at him. "I wouldn't waste my time introducing you either."

"Oh, boy," Clint said from his position leaning against the front of the truck. "I'm going to head out. See you all later this afternoon. Eva, it was a pleasure." He tipped his hat to her.

"Thank you, Clint. I'm grateful you'd come pick us up so early in the morning."

"Not a problem." Clint gave her a warm smile.

"I volunteered, but Sheriff Clint was having none of that," Easton threw in.

"Eva deserved at least a moment's reprieve before meeting you," Clint tossed back.

"A girl does have to prepare herself for charm such as mine." Easton didn't seem offended at all. "Watch out, brothers. Let me show you how a real man impresses Eva Chevron." He swaggered down the steps and toward her, sticking out his hand.

Miles rolled his eyes, and the other brothers groaned.

"Oh my," Mama Millie said.

Eva was amused, but she knew Easton's type—overconfident, flirtatious, and he knew ninety-nine percent of women would swoon when he looked their way. "Nice to meet you," she said, shaking his hand.

"I know it is." Easton winked.

"And who is your incredibly handsome twin?" Eva asked, smiling over at Walker.

A gradual, show-stopping grin lit up the twin's face as everyone but Easton laughed. Walker hurried down the steps and strode over. "Walker Coleville, ma'am. It is truly an honor."

"The honor is all mine," she said as she shook his hand and batted her eyelashes. "I hear you're the best steer roper in all ten states."

"What?" Easton burst out, glaring at Miles. "You showed her roping videos and not me bull riding?"

Miles chuckled. "I'm going to escort Eva to her room now, let her get away from you two and get some much-needed rest."

"Yes, you do that." Mama bustled up the porch steps in front of them.

"Nice to meet you all." Eva lifted a hand to Miles's brothers and dad as they walked past.

"You too," his dad and Walker said. Clint lifted a hand and pulled open his truck door. Interesting he'd said goodbye but had waited. Wanting to watch the drama Easton created or dispel it?

"I'll be seeing you in my dreams, Eva," Easton called as Miles held the front door for her, her small suitcase in his other hand. "Just like I do every night."

"Knock it off," Clint growled at him. "She was attacked tonight and doesn't need to deal with your stupid lines."

"She was attacked?" Easton yelped. "You just told me about the request on the dark web. Ah, shoot. Eva, I'm sorry."

Eva shook her head. "I'm right as rain. No apologies necessary. Goodnight."

"Night," they all echoed more solemnly.

Eva walked with Miles into an open entry, a staircase in front of them with an office to the right and an archway into a large open room to the left. It smelled of cinnamon and apples baking.

"Why didn't you give me all the details?" Easton asked behind them.

"Why can't you not hit on—"

The door shut on Clint's words. Probably for the best. Eva was used to men like Easton hitting on her, but it was kind of Clint to be thoughtful.

"I'm sorry about my boy," Millie said. "He's always a flirt, but put Eva Chevron in front of him and ..." She shrugged.

"It's fine." She was used to flirtations and over-the-top come-ons. "Really. Thank you for opening your home to me. It's lovely and smells delicious."

"Ah, thank you, darlin'. You sure you're not hungry? Thirsty?"

"I'm worn to a frazzle."

"All right then." She nodded to Miles. "Well, hustle her on up to bed. She'll stay in the room we put all the pretty girls in and you'll stay right next to her, not in your cabin. Sorry, love, I know you like a bit of space so Lily ..." She trailed off and looked from Eva to Miles.

Eva's stomach turned over. Lily ... what? Did 'his girl' stay at Miles's cabin?

"It's great. Thank you, Mama." Miles kissed his mama's cheek, then escorted Eva up the stairs with one hand on her lower back and one hand holding the suitcase.

She thrived on his touch and that was a very bad thing for

her. Now that they were here, would he stick close by Eva's side or sneak away to meet Lily at his cabin every chance he got? Her head pounded.

They walked down a wide hallway.

"Mama and Dad's room is downstairs along with the living areas, kitchen, an office for the ranch, and a security center," Miles explained. "There are four suites up here and a game room and theater."

An open door on the left showed a king-sized bed with plush white and gray bedding and pillows.

Miles set the suitcase inside the door and stepped back, gesturing to her. "The room for the pretty girls."

"You've had a lot, I take it?" She leaned into the doorframe, tired but not wanting to say goodnight to him. What was wrong with her?

"I've had …" His brow furrowed. "Oh, you mean we've had numerous ladies stay here for protection details?"

"Yes, *that's* what I meant."

His blue eyes showed he knew she'd been trying to pry out details.

"Aiden dropped Jacey Oliver Miller's name," he said. "Her brother Quaid is a close friend of mine. We used to be in the same unit. Before Jacey, we had a few protection details come through, mostly Clint helping out his buddy with the FBI or something with the sheriff's office. When I explained to my family we had to hide Jacqueline Oliver from her fake and twisted nightmare of a mother, my dad and Clint completely upped the game."

"How so?"

"My dad has trained all of us for as long as I can remember to shoot, fight, pay attention to detail, strategize. He was a Green

Beret." He pushed a hand through his hair. "That's why Clint and I both went into our careers."

"That's impressive."

"Thank you. When Jacey came, he and Clint got busy replacing some of the ranch hands with retired military, and training all the hands so they could double as security guards. They took the perimeter fence from something that either looked good or kept animals in or out to eight feet tall, barbed wire at the top, electric. Quaid had Aiden send him all the latest in security sensors, cameras, and other protections. Lieutenant Hays West, Elizabeth Oliver's current protector, explored the entire property and made certain nobody was getting in without our permission."

"Wow." She didn't know who Lieutenant Hays West was, but everybody knew Elizabeth Oliver, the former senate candidate who had disappeared when her father was exposed for being an underhanded and brilliant criminal and frustratingly escaped arrest and hadn't been found.

He leaned a bit closer. "We can and will keep you safe, Eva."

"Thank you."

He nodded. "I'm also sorry about Easton. I'll talk to him."

"It's fine, Miles. Do you have any clue how many men hit on me like a bunch of cocksure roosters crowing for a chance?" The line had come out as too cocky, but he needed to know she wasn't some wimpy girl. She was from Wyoming, first of all, but she'd had to scrap and fight to succeed in one of the toughest industries in the nation. She could handle putting a guy in his place.

"I don't want to imagine," he said softly. His blue eyes looked pained.

That made her mad. "I'm sure you don't," she snipped back.

He could have his Lily. It wasn't as if she was hurting for male attention. But why did this male seem so ideal? Lieutenant Miles Coleville felt as if he should be hers.

"You handled him well," he said.

"Lots of practice. If Easton is the champion bull rider, I'm the champion male-rejecter." She gave him a challenging look, but she didn't much like the way she was acting or this conversation.

"Hmm." Miles held her gaze for so long, she wanted to look away. She didn't. He studied her as if he would pry past her tough veneer. Finally, he tilted his chin up. "I hope you can rest well. If I'm not out here waiting for you when you wake up, please rap on my door. I'd like you to stay by my side at all times. Even though the ranch hands are exceptionally trained and trustworthy and will be on high alert knowing we're guarding a VIP, there's no reason for them to know Eva Chevron is here. We'll clear areas before I take you anywhere, even on the ranch."

"All right. Goodnight."

She felt his eyes on her as she walked in. She turned as she closed the door. His blue eyes lit a fire of longing inside her chest. That wasn't fair of him at all. She slammed the door in his face.

"Stay by my side at all times," she snipped. "He can stay by his Lily's side for all I care."

She'd said the words much too loud. He'd probably overheard. Pushing out a heavy breath, she blamed her out-of-control longings for a man she couldn't have on exhaustion. It had been a very long, disturbing, and yet thrilling day. How could she stop longing for Miles when his touch was enchanted and his blue eyes stirred something in her soul she never thought she'd feel?

She sank to her knees next to the bed. "Please help me sort this out in my head," she begged heaven above. "I'm not seeing anything clearly right now."

Who knew how much later she awoke, splayed against the side of the bed. Her knees hurt, and she had no answers. Miles Coleville was her rescuer, and he was also the biggest temptation and pain in her backside she'd ever encountered.

Lord give me strength, she muttered mentally, standing and walking to the bathroom. She would try to sleep in for a very long time tomorrow.

CHAPTER
Nine

MILES TEXTED his twin brothers to please wake him if Eva left her room and to send him the links for the cameras and sensors. He got a thumbs-up from Walker and all the information poured in, followed quickly by a text from Easton.

Sorry, bro. Clint didn't give me all the details. All I heard was Eva Chevron. Sorry I acted insensitive.

Miles could only imagine the tongue-lashing Easton had gotten from Mama. She doted on her boys but didn't accept 'ill behavior'.

It's all right. Apparently she has millions of men coming onto her every day. Nothing you did or said bothered her.

It all bothered him. He and Clint being at odds bothered him. That wasn't typical for them. Clint was put out for Lily's sake. It was typical for the sheriff to think he needed to protect everybody, but he seemed overly worried about Lily. Which made him wonder if there was something more to Lily's tears six months ago and maybe Clint knew about it. He had to get to the bottom of that soon.

Eva having 'lots of practice and being the champion male-rejecter' bothered Miles as well. The words he hoped he'd misconstrued through the closed door made his stomach squirm. '… stay by Lily's side for all I care.'

This was sticky. He wanted to get back to the interactions with Eva before he had stupidly stopped a kiss between them and told her he had a girl.

Was that even possible? Maybe he had ruined something great before it even began. He didn't see an alternate path, though. If he had it to do over, he had no idea how he'd change it.

He got ready for bed, said his prayers, and didn't set an alarm. His brothers, dad, and the foreman would monitor the security, and he'd hear a beep if an alert came in.

Sunshine streamed into the room when he awoke. He checked his phone. It was seven-ten. Sleeping in for him, but still pretty early. Especially as they'd arrived after two.

He listened for sounds of movement next door and heard nothing. Rushing to shower and get ready, he went to the closet to open his duffel bag but noticed his mama had moved clothes from his cabin here. He'd dumped his bag in the closet, too tired and stirred up over Eva to notice anything last night.

He smiled—Carhartt and Ariat T-shirts, Wrangler and Ariat jeans, Justin and Tecovas boots, and some of his favorite Stetson hats. He'd brought some of his cowboy wear to base. It made him a bit unique, and it was his personality and identity to a certain extent, but for the most part if he wasn't in his Navy uniform or issued gear, he wore casual T-shirts, joggers, and running shoes like everybody else.

Dressing in his favorite Ariat T-shirt and jeans, he pulled his Tecovas on, grabbed his Stetson hat, and headed out the bedroom door. He paused in the hallway. He'd felt empowered charging out here, but now he had nothing to do but wait. He'd been on plenty of details where he had to be motionless, monitor, and wait for hours or days on end. He didn't love them. He should've used the gym out in the barn before he showered and got ready, but he didn't want to be too far from Eva.

Hat in his hands, he paced the hall outside Eva's door. He thought he heard movement. He paused and ... nothing. The scents of bacon and sweet pancakes drifted up, and his stomach growled. Though he doubted he'd ever move back to Coleville, he missed his family and his home. Being here was great. Mama's food was the whipped cream on top of the experience.

Miles resumed his pacing. He could go down and eat and she'd probably still be sleeping, but he wanted to be here, wanted to see her. He pushed a hand through his hair.

Footsteps thudded up the stairs.

Walker. Of course. His most thoughtful brother—well, besides Houston. Houston was the youngest and being thoughtful stopped the brothers from picking on him. It was also most likely a requirement for a doctor to be thoughtful.

"Hey, bro. Mama wondered why you're wearing a hole in the ceiling. I said I'd come check to protect you from her cussin' you." He gave his slow grin.

"Thanks."

"Sure. So ..."

Miles shrugged, gesturing to Eva's door. "I want to be here when she wakes up."

"I can understand that. Eva Chevron." He let out a whistle. "Mama gave Easton the what-for. He should calm down now.

It's just ... Eva Chevron." He lifted his hands and smiled. "How long have we all crushed on her?"

"A long time," Miles admitted, turning his hat in his hands. How to explain it was more than a crush for him? She was brave, kind, and perfect for him. They had a mind-altering, future-changing connection... that he couldn't act on. He hung his head.

"All the pictures all over your cabin." Walker chuckled. "That ticked Lily off." His smile faded. "What are you going to do about her? She deserves to be free."

"I want her to be. I've got to go see her." He shrugged. "See if I can figure it out without hurting her." He wasn't getting into Lily and all his issues right outside Eva's door. She was more than likely still asleep, but ... what if?

"I'll try to help you make that happen. Lily's amazing, but any fool can see you two aren't meant to be." Walker pointed at the door and lowered his voice. "Meant to be?"

"I've probably messed it up already."

"How so?" Walker leaned against the wall, not in any hurry. He had a way of studying you and making you feel like whatever you were saying was the most important thing in the world to him.

"Will she ever believe that she's special and not just because she's famous? I made the mistake of saying something about Lily. I've never been a mess like this." He realized he wasn't making a lot of sense.

"You've got some time to be around Eva. If it's right, it'll work out. Besides, I've never known a woman who wasn't into you. The Navy SEAL thing is the clincher." He grinned.

"The championship roper and cowboy grin isn't working for you?" Miles teased.

"It works just fine. I have plenty of women chasing me, just not ... the one I can't get out of my head." He rubbed at his jaw. "Do you think you'll finally ... close that chapter of your life?" There was a hopeful light in his eyes. Was Miles right in assuming Walker had a crush on Lily? Was she the one Walker couldn't get out of his head?

"I have to be a lot firmer about it than last time."

"You do that."

"Any vested interest in me doing that?"

Walker raised his eyebrows but didn't comment.

"Even if I do end things, it might be too late to make a play for Eva."

"I don't know. I saw how she looked at you, how she leaned into you." Walker splayed his hands. "See you downstairs in a bit."

"Thanks, Walker."

Walker tilted his chin and strode off. A few minutes later, soft footsteps sounded in Eva's room. He perked up and wondered if he should lean against the wall and put the cowboy hat on, try to imitate Clint's patented John Wayne look. He shook his head at himself. He didn't posture, and Walker was right. Women were drawn to him. He'd always kept his distance because of Lily. Now he had to somehow walk a line because of Lily. How soon could he go meet with her and end the relationship? How horrible was that of him? He wouldn't have stepped up if he hadn't met Eva. He kept justifying that it was better for Lily.

The door behind him creaked open.

Miles turned and his mouth gaped open wider than the door. He reminded himself to flap it closed as he clung tightly to his hat. She was in a simple, soft-looking knee-length T-shirt dress. It wasn't clingy or revealing or anything. Eva didn't need to show off. She was more appealing than any woman he'd ever seen, and it had nothing to do with her fame or her acting ability. He didn't even think it had much to do with her gorgeous face. It was how real she was, how they connected, her bravery, the sparks and draw he felt between them, the light that shone from her face, the kindness that was instinctively hers but he imagined she'd worked throughout her life to cultivate.

"Morning," he managed. He had a moment of terror when she didn't respond. Had she overheard his conversation with Walker? Did she hate him and think he was two-timing his 'girl back home'?

Her gaze traveled over him, and she looked as breathless as he felt. "Good morning," she said. Then she grinned, and the floor shifted under his feet. He spread his stance. It helped. A bit. That grin restored his faith that he had a chance with her. Walker would help him; he would watch diligently over Eva while Miles found Lily and broke things off. Would Easton flirt with Eva and try to get her to fall for him while Miles was gone? No, he would try that regardless of where Miles was. Hopefully Clint would be busy with sheriff duties and not get in on the competition.

"Bacon and real pancakes." She gave an exaggerated inhale and then a sigh. "Do you know how long it's been since I've had real pancakes?" She pinned him with a threatening look. "Do not tell my trainer."

"You got it." He offered an elbow. "Breakfast?"

"Oh no." She tugged at the hem of the T-shirt, nightgown, whatever she was wearing. "I've got to clean up. Get dressed. If the paparazzi catch you un-pretty and without makeup on, dressed in something comfortable you can actually sleep in …"

She made a choking sound low in her throat, grasping at her pretty neck.

Miles chuckled and could not resist stepping up close to her. "Eva, I've got some news for you."

She tilted her head back and her lips parted. She moistened them, and every system in his body revved into overdrive. How was he supposed to resist this perfect-for-him-woman?

Throughout the past twelve years on his visits home, he had spent time with Lily and wasn't tempted to touch her, hadn't even thought about it. They'd sit shoulder to shoulder watching a movie, then he'd give her a perfunctory hug or kiss at the end of the night and feel the comfort of being close to a long-time friend.

With Eva, he couldn't stand to be a foot away. His good friend Quaid Raven had told him when he met Anna he had every reason to fight the draw to her, most of all Anna's safety from his demented mother, and still he'd been unable to resist her at times. That's how he felt with Eva after less than a day of knowing her. She was irresistible to him.

"What news is that?" she asked.

"Well, first of all, you aren't going to be seeing any paparazzi for a bit."

"Yes!" She punched both fists in the air and almost knocked him in the chin.

He chuckled, set his hat on a decorated side table, and wrapped both hands around her small, clenched fists. He tucked her hands against his chest. Every touch with her was natural, incredible, thrilling.

Her breath shortened and her hands softened within his grasp. He rubbed his thumbs across the back of her hands and lost his train of thought. He feared she'd pull away, but she seemed interested in him, not leery as she'd been at times last night.

"So what you're saying is I can wear this comfy nightshirt around, with my hair in tangles and no makeup on, pull faces at Easton, eat real pancakes with homemade syrup, and nobody is going to snap a picture and go viral on the internet or splay it on the rag tags at the grocery store checkout line?"

"Yes, ma'am. That is what I'm saying." He kept rubbing his thumbs along the backs of her hands, mesmerized by her dark eyes and how perfectly her hands fit in his.

"And what was the second thing?" Her dark eyes sparkled with anticipation.

"Second thing?"

"You said first of all," she reminded him. "That generally intones there's a second of all."

He chuckled.

"I'd like to hear more. Since you're giving me fabulous news that is counteracting the fact that I'm hunted by faceless and menacing gnomes who reside in the dark web."

He laughed even harder. "Has anyone ever told you that you're delightful?"

"Oh, all the time." She winked. "But I've never heard that word from the lips of a Navy SEAL cowboy hero. I like the new look, by the way."

"Thank you. It's actually the old look. Personally, I'm a fan of the comfy nightshirt look."

"Are you now? You can thank Autumn later."

"I will make that a priority." Miles was in so much trouble. He had two choices currently—kiss Eva, or run to find Lily and break it off and then return and kiss Eva. He had to go with option number two. He had to. His body rebelled against him, edging closer. *Stay strong*, he begged himself. By tonight he could be a free man. If he had his way, he'd be a committed to Eva man, and he'd be thrilled to end his freedom moments after he proclaimed it. Captured by Eva sounded like the best state a man could be in.

"So, number two?" She smiled as if him constantly losing his train of thought around her was a normal and natural thing. It was, but he wasn't used to it. He was the lieutenant; he was in charge. His words were obeyed. He didn't have the luxury of losing his train of thought. This crazy situation they'd been thrown into was a break for him in a way, too. Aiden, Autumn, Paul and Aiden's tech team were doing the hard work while he relaxed and focused on Eva.

"Number two." He drew in a breath and knew he should hold these thoughts until he was officially broken up with Lily. He'd been described as the most 'pathetically-loyal long-distance boyfriend' in history by many of his buddies in the military and his brothers. He'd been proud of his loyalty, worn it like a badge until it started poking him in the chest, the guilty thoughts constantly nagging at him that Lily needed to be free and move on, even if she didn't realize it.

Right now he wanted to switch those loyalties to Eva. Would she believe him when he explained it all, or would it upset her? She'd been upset at Aiden's when he didn't kiss her and admitted he had a girl back home. Right now, she wasn't upset. Her eyes sparkled, her lips were soft, and she was close enough he could smell her sweet coconut scent.

"Number two," he repeated, and let his gaze sweep over her face. "You couldn't look 'un-pretty' if you tried. Your beauty is natural and shines from the inside out because of your kindness and genuineness and the light of Christ that radiates from you."

Eva studied him and then her lower lip trembled. Miles wanted to kiss that lip desperately. "That might be the nicest thing anyone has ever said to me."

Miles almost scoffed at that. She was heralded for her beauty and talent by media and talk show hosts around the world. She was desired by every man he knew, except his dad and his married friends. She was the most beautiful woman the world over. He held his tongue because he knew she was sincere in her response, and he would never scoff at her.

"Eva ..." His voice was gravelly. "I would love to say much nicer things to you, morning, noon, and night."

She smiled at him. It lit up the already-bright morning.

Without warning, her smile dropped. "There's a but ..." She jerked her hands free and backed into the bedroom. "I'm so sorry. I got caught up in the moment and you and ..." She rubbed at her forehead. "I forgot about your girl. Lily. She's here. In Coleville. Right? I'm so sorry. And ..." Her face tightened and her eyes filled with frustration. "You should be more sorry." She slammed the door in his face.

Miles studied the door. She was right. He should be more sorry. He was the one with a long-time commitment he hadn't been able to rescind. He lost his mind around Eva, and he'd never acted like that before. It wasn't fair to her or Lily.

He scrubbed at his chin. He was making a mess of all of this. It wasn't like they taught relationship classes in BUD/S, so how was he supposed to navigate this type of troubled water? Somehow, today, he had to find Lily and end the relationship once and for all. It would hurt, but it would be for the best in the long run.

As soon as it was finished, and he helped Lily however he could, Miles would storm up to Eva and proclaim his freedom and his intentions toward her. He would cup her face, kiss her for a very long time, and talk everything out.

Miles groaned and leaned against the wall. In a perfect world, that was what would happen. In his world, he feared the ending would be more doors slammed in his face.

CHAPTER Ten

EVA KEPT a practiced smile on her face and fought her darndest to stay in character and stay detached from Miles. She'd loved relaxing and being herself around him. Now she'd have to utilize her acting skills to guard her heart. The problem was she couldn't decide what role to play. A forbidden romance would just make her long for him more. She couldn't force herself to pretend he was a double agent or a secretly evil character. She finally decided she'd have to stick with the truth—he was off limits, and she refused to be the woman who broke up a relationship.

His family helped distract her. Mama Millie fussed over her during breakfast. Easton and Walker tripped over themselves complimenting her and trying to take care of her every need.

The problem was, Miles was right there. He looked like the cowboy slash military hero she'd always longed to find, but he wasn't some poster boy or movie character. This was Miles. He was genuine, humble, true, and the electricity in the air between them was difficult to ignore. The yearning in his brilliant blue eyes was even worse.

He had kept some distance from her after she slammed the door in his face. He didn't take her hand or put his hand on the small of her back as they walked down to breakfast, ate with Easton, Walker, Jared, and Millie, and pitched in to clean up. Not touching helped. No, not really. Nothing helped. How soon would he run for his Lily?

Eva dried the dishes Miles handed to her from rinsing, trying to avoid touching his too-intriguing hands every time. She hadn't washed dishes by hand since she'd been home to Wyoming. She liked it.

When they were done, Miles got a FaceTime call from Autumn on his phone. She had hardly said hello to Eva and Miles when Easton popped his head into the picture behind Eva.

"Well, hello handsome," Autumn purred. "Are you the one and only Easton Coleville? Bull rider extraordinaire and my future boyfriend?"

Easton's face broke into a huge grin. It appeared he had to remind himself to act suave. He gave Autumn a smoldering look. "Yes, ma'am, I am. You have me at a disadvantage, beautiful. I would love to hear your name and when we're going to meet in person."

Autumn chuckled, low and throaty. "As soon as I can hunt down the scum threatening my friend Eva and dismantle them, you plan on a date."

"You'll hunt them down and dismantle them?" Easton whooped. "I think I've met the love of my life."

Autumn laughed again. "You're irresistible, but just so you're up to speed, the term boyfriend was stretching it. Love of my life will never happen. I'm not available for anything but shallow hookups."

Easton's eyes widened.

"Now I have heard about enough of this bull-larky," Mama Millie sputtered from across the kitchen where she'd been wiping down the table. She slammed both palms on the wood tabletop. "Young lady," she threatened. "You had better ask our dear Savior to help you find a moral compass, and don't you even think the words 'shallow hookup' regarding one of my boys again. Do I make myself clear?"

Miles and Eva exchanged a look. Mama was a sweetheart—until you pushed the wrong button, apparently. Jared and Walker both grimaced.

"Forgive me, Mama," Easton said.

"I had no idea your mother was in the room," Autumn said, her eyes darting around wildly, trying to see Mama or look for an escape route. "Please forgive me, Mrs. Coleville."

"Of course I will, and I will pray for you to find the love of Jesus in your life." Mama's voice was much softer.

"Um ... thank you?" Autumn looked desperate to escape. "Miles and Eva, should I call later, or can we talk in private?"

"We can talk in private now," Miles reassured her. "Excuse us," he said to everyone in the room. He took Eva's elbow and directed her out of the kitchen, through the living room and the entryway and into the office.

The ranch foreman was in the security room. He lifted a hand. Eva liked the quiet man. He seemed to spend more time in the security center than taking care of the ranch. Jared helped him with both the ranch work and the security center.

Miles shut the office door behind them and he and Eva stood

side by side, looking into his phone screen and Autumn's pinched face.

"You all right?" Miles asked.

"I should be asking you two that," Autumn insisted.

"We're doing just fine," Miles answered, then looked to Eva.

She'd be more than fine if he were a free man. That was hardly the question. "Yes. We got settled in and slept, just had breakfast. Nothing dangerous here."

"Besides Mama defending her boy," Autumn snipped.

Miles bristled.

Before he could open his mouth, Autumn rushed on, "Forgive me, Miles. She had every right and I'm sure she's an angelic mother. I had no clue she was there and was just flirting but setting my boundaries like I always do."

"A shallow hookup is a boundary?" Miles asked.

Eva wondered how Miles would survive in Hollywood. Most of the time, nobody was honest enough to admit to a shallow hookup, but that was all anyone seemed to want.

"I never do more than kiss any man." Autumn's smile got sneaky and much more like the Autumn Eva had met last night. "When they make any move to do more, I knock them on their butts. It's so fun."

Miles half-grunted and shook his head. "My brother would never try to do more."

"Whew. That man is more appealing by the moment. Except for the fact he still lives with his mama."

"He doesn't. He has his own cabin."

"Yes! Sign me up for a flirting and kissing session with my bull riding cowboy very soon."

"Autumn." Miles half-laughed now. "You are a very impressive lady, and a piece of work. Do you know that?"

"Yes, Lieutenant Coleville, I do." Her voice turned hard. "Now, enough about me. You're safe there from your perspective?"

"Yes."

"Our reports are revealing some of the media and Eva's friends and work associates are buying the sick in bed line and some are not."

Eva wondered who wasn't buying the sickness. It was disconcerting not to have her phone and respond to family, friends, and work associates and know what the media was saying.

"I don't look enough like Eva to venture outside," Autumn continued, "which is going to drive me insane by the way, but that's all right. More motivation to catch these losers and restore Eva and me to our happy lives. Anyway, I've spotted a few prowlers in the night, but like the good girl I am, I followed Aiden's instructions and didn't leave the house. Paul found a VRBO a few doors down and across the street. No beach views for the poor guy. He's checking in at four and will be able to go after anybody prowling around tonight."

She took a breath. "This morning has been interesting. Some stiff in a white uniform knocked on the door. I figured if I pulled him into the house and didn't let him see my face, I could see what he was about—"

"Autumn," Eva broke in. "Oh, shoot. I should've told you my chef delivers meals on Tuesday mornings."

"Eh." Autumn lifted her hands and grinned. "It gave me something to do, and he was surprisingly chill about it. I explained I'd learned how to take a man down in *Protecting the Influencer*."

"He never saw your face?" Miles asked.

"No, sir. To more exciting news. I was in the shower when our buddy Agent Ryken Henderson decided to disable the alarms and stroll in the house like he owned the place."

Eva's blood chilled. "Are you serious?"

"Deadly serious. He came right into the master. Aiden has Adam tailing him, and I had alerts going off that he was coming so luckily I'd jumped out of the shower and got a robe on and a weapon in hand. Not that I'd need a weapon to take out that pansy. We had a nice conversation through the master bathroom door. I convinced him I was miserably sick, probably had the worst flu virus I'd ever had in my life. I kept sneezing and coughing and sniffling. He kept fishing for why the camera feeds weren't working. Scum ball didn't want to openly admit he was watching you on camera. I must've convinced him he wasn't getting answers and he didn't want the gumbo. He left. Adam said he's gone to work. I'm fighting Aiden for permission to just thrash him when he comes back. Easiest way to get the truth out of a loser like that."

Miles smiled at Eva. "Aiden sticks to a code of ethics."

"Blah, blah, blah," Autumn said. "You want ethical or you want the innocent to be protected? Agent Henderson doesn't give two rats about ethics." She waved a hand. "Anyway. Aiden, Paul, and the tech team are all focused on unraveling who put the hits out on the dark web. It still looks to be seven different parties, but that doesn't mean they aren't all related or trace back to one slime ball. Any questions or ideas from your end?"

Eva looked at Miles and lifted her hands. "Besides Ryken, I don't know anybody who is after me."

"Besides the millions of men around the globe who are in love with Eva Chevron," Miles said.

"So it could be anyone," Eva said, wondering if she misread

the jealousy in Miles's voice. She didn't like when he said her full name, as if she were the famous actress and an object, not a real woman with feelings. Feelings for *him*.

"You haven't dated anyone seriously, from the media's standpoint, besides Lake Eastwood for years," Autumn interjected. "Correct?"

"Yes."

"Lake Eastwood." Autumn whistled long and low. "Now there is a fine piece of man flesh."

Miles stiffened.

"He's a lot better looking on the outside than on the inside," Eva said.

Miles visibly relaxed.

"Truly?" Autumn's smooth brow wrinkled. "Everybody adores him. You two were the couple of the century, I swear."

"I'm not sure how you missed the media hailstorm, but Lake cheated on me with Bermuda Venus and Jezebel Noir," Eva admitted, not looking at Miles. It had been humiliating enough when it happened.

"The scum!" Autumn cried out. The video went wild as she paced around in a circle. "I can't! I must've been on a deep cover assignment. I just assumed you broke up. I loathe him! Cheating on Eva Chevron. What kind of a loser ... Miles, you must avenge her!"

"Gladly," Miles gritted out.

Eva let herself look at him. His fists and jaw were clenched and the muscles in his arms were all engaged. She wished her cowboy hero could avenge her. But he wasn't hers.

"Has the idiot tried to get you back?" Autumn asked.

"Constantly."

Miles flinched.

"Don't you dare fall for his lies," Autumn warned.

Eva barked out a laugh. "Don't worry, friend. I would never let him get in my head again."

"Good." There was a pause, then Autumn asked, "Have you had any interaction with him recently?"

"When he found out Jorge was after me, he found me and demanded that I call him if I was in danger." She rolled her eyes. "As if his fake muscles could protect me."

She glanced at Miles again. His very real muscles had protected her. She wanted to lean into his solidness and forget about all this stress for a while.

"What did you tell him?" Autumn asked.

"I told him to drop dead in the ditch and I'd rather pick up a rattlesnake." She smiled to herself. "Then he said to me, 'Don't think your Idaho redneck lingo is going to win you any roles without me. You'll be crawling back and begging me to love you again.'"

"Pardon me?" Miles turned to her. "He threatened you and the idiot doesn't even know where you're from?"

"It doesn't matter." She shrugged but loved that Miles got how annoying that was. "My producer and agent won't listen if he tries to blackball me. From what I've heard, Jezebel and Bermuda want nothing to do with him and his lying tongue either. He's burning his own bridges."

There was a pause, then Miles asked, "How did he find out Jorge was after you?"

Eva searched her brain, trying to remember. She'd been irritated when he showed up at the gym as she was exiting the private training room. "I remember asking him and he skirted the answer, kept talking about how concerned he was for me and how he wanted to be there for me. He only said his last lines after I wouldn't give in to his 'charm'."

"Doesn't sound very charming," Miles muttered.

Eva agreed but said nothing.

He pushed out a breath and focused on Autumn. "We'll relay this to Aiden, but keep an eye out for Lake."

"Oh, I will." Autumn smiled. "He sounds like a fun one to lure in, then almost break an arm."

"I think that would be a great lesson for him," Eva agreed.

"But keep the objective in mind," Miles said. "We want everyone believing Eva is home sick in bed and we want information from Lake, not a broken arm."

"I said 'almost a broken arm'," Autumn reminded him. "I know, I know. Nobody will see this gorgeous face and realize it's not the famous and gorgeous face of my friend Eva." She smiled, but then her golden eyes became penetrating. "Eva. Are you doing okay emotionally? You feel safe and comfortable there?"

Eva's throat felt thick. "Thank you for asking. I'm very safe and comfortable here." She risked a glance at Miles. "Emotionally, I'm trying not to think about some weird bounty on my head. Thank you for all you're doing to figure this out."

"I'd say it's my job, but I have too much fun to consider it work." Autumn grinned. "All right. I'm signing off. Chat soon."

"Bye," Miles and Eva both echoed.

Miles turned to her, and Eva's heart immediately picked up its beat with one searching look from those blue eyes. "I apologize. I haven't asked how you're doing emotionally."

"You're a guy and my bodyguard. I don't think my emotional state is part of your job description."

He looked over her face. "I wish it could be."

Eva's eyes widened and her stomach pitched happily. Just as quickly, it dropped. It couldn't be his job. He had Lily.

"You deserve much better than some idiot like Lake who doesn't appreciate the real you and would cheat on you," Miles said softly.

Eva studied him. Did he think he knew the real her? Did he want to? Did she need to remind him about his 'girl back home'?

Miles suddenly stiffened and pulled his phone out. "Aiden," he said.

She nodded and listened in as he shared with Aiden about Lake. Aiden agreed to check into him. Aiden talked about some of the technology they were using to track the individuals who'd made the requests on the dark web.

At least the threat to her life gave her a small distraction from the threat to her heart.

CHAPTER Eleven

AFTER THEY HUNG up with Aiden, they found Easton and Walker waiting in the foyer for them. The four of them went on a long horseback ride around their property. Eva wore a hat and sunglasses in case they ran into any of the ranch hands. Easton explained their workers were trained guards as well and wouldn't rat her out, but it was just smarter to have fewer people know *the* Eva Chevron was here.

She'd never say anything to Miles's brother, but it was irritating when somebody called her *the* Eva Chevron. She was proud of her acting talent and prowess, but she wanted to be seen for herself, for her heart. Miles seemed to see her that way. Not that it could matter.

It was wonderful to be on a horse again and the ranch was picturesque, large, and intriguing. For all intents and purposes, the Colevilles appeared to be wealthy ranchers protecting their prized Brahman bulls with the huge fence and security guards. What guests didn't see was the security center, the fact that every ranch hand doubled as a guard, was heavily armed, and how well-trained at fighting and with weapons these cowboys were.

Easton and Walker told her more about Jacey Oliver's stay with them and how they went to check on Jacey and Cade Miller's property up the canyon now that the newlyweds were in hiding because the nefarious Benjamin Oliver was still at large. They told her about Elizabeth Oliver staying here as well and her heroic boyfriend Lieutenant Hays West swimming up that very river and proving a criminal could get in that way. They now had a very secure grate under said river. Lieutenant West was coincidentally best friends with Shawn Holister and the deceased Mercedes Belle. It didn't bother Eva that they name-dropped. She'd met the sweetheart Mercedes before and the Viking Warrior Shawn.

They stopped at the side of the lake and the rope swing Elizabeth Oliver had swung off of. The men stripped off their shirts and slid out of their cowboy boots, set their weapons down, and swung in wearing their jeans.

Eva reminded herself she wasn't dating Miles and had never been into 'shallow hookups' like Autumn had teased about. She shouldn't make Miles an object and gawk at him without a shirt on. But there was well-built, and there was beautiful, and Miles's upper body was eons past both. He was a work of art. She closed her eyes, but it didn't matter. The image of his tanned skin and muscular body were imprinted in her mind.

Not to be outdone by the famed Elizabeth Oliver, the ice queen, Eva swung into the lake in her T-shirt and shorts. It was exhilarating and chilly. She liked the look of appreciation in Miles's eyes, before she reminded herself about Lily for the twentieth time in an hour.

Poor Lily. Did the woman know Miles was a two-timer? Eva would never have believed it herself if she wasn't the one the enticing Navy SEAL was looking at so earnestly. Miles seemed too loyal, from 'good stock' as her dad would say. The way his mom had reacted, and even Easton's wide eyes at Autumn's 'shallow hookup' comment, made her believe Miles would feel the same. Was he only interested in her as a bodyguard? He was a diligent bodyguard, but he'd also leaned in and almost kissed her and touched her more than was necessary to do his job. She couldn't riddle him out.

They returned their horses to the stables after they finished their ride around the ranch. Easton and Walker wanted her to tour their cabins.

They made it to Miles's cabin. The space was as manly and appealing as he was. It was set up similar to his brothers', with two levels, a wide front porch, rustic beams supporting the porch overhang, and lots of windows. The main level was an open living area with a laundry room and half bath, the upstairs a small loft area extending over the living room. Off the loft was a master suite and two extra bedrooms with a bath between them.

She couldn't stop envisioning him and Lily cuddled in the front porch swing, on the couch, in his bed ... Her face flared red, and her gut churned. Did he sleep with Lily in this cabin? There wasn't a trace of anything feminine and she had noticed how religious the Colevilles were. Not only did they pray at breakfast, but they talked about the Bible and their Savior. They had beautiful works of art in the living room and office of the Savior. What did that mean to Miles, though? Not every child followed the path of their parents.

"Why did you build a cabin here if you're rarely home?" she

asked him as they finished the tour and stood out on the porch, savoring the view of mountains covered with pine and aspen trees to the east. Had he built it for Lily?

"Rhett built it, not me. He had a designer come up with the plans for Easton, Walker, and several other cabins. He insisted it was easy to build another cookie-cutter for me." Miles shrugged. "I couldn't tell him no. The cabin gets used for protection details, and I usually stay here when I visit."

Eva liked the layout and openness of each of these cabins. It didn't feel cookie-cutter. Her house on the beach was built similar to several along the same stretch. It probably did save the builder money and time.

He 'usually stayed here' and Mama had said something about Lily in regard to Miles's cabin. Eva might be sick.

"Are you never gonna move back home?" Walker asked, his hat clenched in his hands as the men always removed their hats inside, just like her dad and uncles would. Being around the Colevilles made her miss her family.

"Not in the foreseeable future." Miles held his brother's gaze. "I love you all and miss you, but being a SEAL is my calling in life."

They studied each other. The tension grew, and Eva couldn't help but wonder if this was about Miles not coming back to his family or not coming back for Lily. What if some of his brothers wanted Lily to be their sister-in-law or maybe to be free so they could pursue her?

"Mama's texting that lunch is ready," Easton interrupted.

Eva regarded Miles as they walked off the porch and back toward the main house for lunch. Was his 'girl back home' just an excuse he gave to keep all the women off of him? No, there was a Lily. His brothers had all mentioned her. Did Lily not care that Miles wasn't moving back home anytime soon? Why didn't they marry? Why hadn't she moved near his home base? Her mind spun with questions, and she refused to voice any of them.

Lily felt like the elephant in the room between them. Still, Eva had to keep reminding herself about the woman. Miles seemed completely invested in Eva. Maybe she was reading it wrong again. He was focused on her as a bodyguard and she kept believing he was staring at her, giving her longing looks, laughing at things she said more than his brothers and family did.

Before she ate, Eva hurried upstairs and changed into a pretty pale blue sundress, ran a brush through her hair, and put on some lip gloss and lotion. Makeup seemed overdone in this fresh air location, and when Miles gave her the most appreciative glance as she walked out of her bedroom door, she didn't think he cared about makeup.

Lunch was delicious—taco salad—and loud with Easton and Walker telling her stories about their rodeo successes and showing her videos. They were good guys, and funny, but she was partial to Miles even though she shouldn't be.

After lunch, Millie insisted she and Miles lay down for a spell. Miles protested he hadn't taken a nap since kindergarten, but Millie shooed them up the stairs. "You told me as a SEAL you have to get sleep when you can. You're safe here, you can't do anything to track down the bad people after our darling Eva, and you both look dead on your feet."

She walked them up to their rooms, so Eva didn't get the chance to speak with Miles alone. That was for the best.

She fell asleep quickly but woke to voices and movement in the hallway. Similar to this morning, she heard the low rumble of their voices but couldn't discern the words. Straightening her sundress and smoothing her hair, she hurried to the door and swung it open.

Miles and Clint were both in the hallway, no hats, but they were very similar looking in their T-shirts, jeans, and cowboy boots. The blue eyes all the Coleville boys had inherited from Jared were appealing.

She'd thought Clint looked like a cowboy poster last night. Miles looked even better in the gear.

"Morning, sunshine," Clint drawled.

She patted her hair again. "How long did I sleep?"

"Probably not long enough," Miles said. "Last night was traumatic, and you didn't sleep in much this morning. You've been impressively brave and resilient."

"Thank you." Eva felt the sincerity of his compliment all the way through, backed up by a meaningful look in his blue gaze.

"How are you feeling?" Miles asked.

"Good." She looked between them, sensing that tension she'd felt last night. "What's on the agenda now?"

"I'm going to thump a Navy SEAL in the barn." Clint pumped his eyebrows.

Miles chuckled. "Actually, I'm going to thump the almighty sheriff and not even get a felony for assault and battery."

"You'll try, little bro."

"And I'll win." Miles folded his muscled arms across his chest and gave her a searching look.

Eva had the oddest reaction to this fight, that look in his blue eyes, the obvious strength in his arms. Her stomach hopped happily at the thought of Miles fighting for her. Was that what they were fighting about, or was it for Lily? She had the feeling that at least one of the brothers was interested in Lily. Eva wanted to see the woman, not keep her faceless. At the same time, she never wanted to meet Lily with no last name and no face. If she liked the girl, she'd feel even more guilty. If she didn't like her, she'd wonder why Miles would be committed to her.

"Can I come watch?" she asked.

"I think you'd better, so you know who to turn to in an emergency." Clint offered his arm. "The future champion will escort you."

Miles guffawed. "You haven't beat me in years."

"*Future* champion. I've got skills you've never seen before," Clint flung back.

Eva barked out a laugh. "You two are like a couple of roosters strutting about."

Miles grinned at that. "I am the alpha rooster. The king of the flock, you might say."

Eva laughed again.

"We'll see, little brother. We'll see."

"Let me grab my shoes." Eva hurried back into the room, used the bathroom to freshen up quick, and tied her shoes before rushing back out. "Sorry to make you wait."

"Not a problem, little lady," Clint drawled, offering his elbow again.

Eva slid her arm through the crook, her hand brushing his bicep. It was a nice muscle. He smelled nice, looked nice, seemed like a great guy. But her heart did not skip a beat at his nearness, and no tingly warmth filled her body at one brush of his fingers or longing look from his blue eyes.

Clint was a humble hero similar to Miles, but she'd seen Miles fight to protect her. He'd rescued her from death or worse. He was a Navy SEAL Lieutenant yet still humble in his speech and actions. She was mesmerized by him, no matter how she tried to tamp the feelings down.

Miles didn't say much as he followed them down the stairs. Both men plunked their cowboy hats on and Eva remembered to put her baseball hat and sunglasses back on. They walked out the side door and through Millie's pretty backyard, complete with a trellis, vegetable garden, and flower garden.

The men pecked at each other with verbal jabs as they walked. Eva called them a couple of hens and they both grinned.

Surprisingly, Easton and Walker weren't in the barn. She thought they'd be here as an audience.

"You're my only fan," Clint told her.

Miles growled low in his throat.

"What?" Clint asked, arching an eyebrow. "You should've invited Lily."

Eva's insides froze.

"You know I couldn't do that and risk word spreading about Eva being here." Miles said the line reasonably, but honestly, he looked like he was steaming and ready to flatten his brother. "Let's do this."

The men got ready, removing their shirts, boots, and socks, wrapping their hands, putting on headgear. They both had jeans on, and that struck her as funny. How could they move well in jeans?

As soon as the fight started, she realized the jeans flowed with the men nicely. She'd never seen a fight like this. She remembered seeing fights as a teenager in high school, and she'd seen lots of staged fights for filming. She'd attended boxing and MMA events.

But this? This was a cross between a street fight and a professional boxing match. Miles and Clint were obviously both experts at boxing and MMA style fighting, but there was something more raw about this fight, as if they were trying to prove themselves. She still wasn't certain if it was about Lily, or possibly about herself. Clint hardly knew her, so she doubted it was about her, but then a lot of men didn't know her at all and thought they were her 'future'. The fight could be about brothers who had a past grievance to air, or possibly just brothers slugging it out as she'd heard men liked to do. She and her sisters didn't fight like this.

Easton and Walker wandered into the barn during the battle.

"How long they been at it?" Easton asked.

She lifted her hands, hating to tear her gaze away from the beauty and fluidity of movement Miles had, even as her neck tightened every time Clint got in a vicious hit. "Maybe ten minutes?"

"Just getting started then," Walker said. "Should I go make popcorn?"

Miles and Clint ignored their brothers. They didn't even taunt each other. Miles glanced her direction and got clocked in the head. She cried out and had to clap her hand over her mouth. He stumbled but righted himself quickly.

"He's all right," Walker said. "It would take a lot more than that to down one of my brothers."

Walker was right about that. The two men fought and fought and fought. No hit or kick, no matter how hard, seemed enough to take either of them down.

Walker forced them to take a break and drink the water bottles he had for them, but then he left to help one of the ranch hands fix a fence.

Easton stayed by Eva's side. He gave her play-by-play on the action, sounding like a sports broadcaster but adding in some Walker humor and making her laugh.

"And Clint gets in a solid jab, but Miles rebuttals him with a roundhouse. If either of our contenders possessed my devastatingly handsome looks, they'd worry about their faces being rearranged."

Eva laughed at him, but quietly, not her normal loud bark that used to embarrass her. She owned her laugh now and Miles had said he loved it.

The tension between the two seemed to increase by the minute. Clint bloodied Miles's nose, and Eva cried out. Miles split Clint's lip, and she gasped. The two didn't stop for more water, a rest, or a peace treaty. Even though Easton offered them a peace treaty signing where he would 'mediate while they aired their grievances'.

Jared finally came into the barn and heaved a sigh. "Walker ratted you two out. Millie says you better get your feuding selves cleaned up before dinner. Come on. It's gone on too long. You aren't solving whatever issue you think is between ya tonight."

The brothers backed away from each other, glaring.

"Come on, Eva." Walker tilted his head. "Papa and I will walk you in. I'm sure Mama would love to see you."

"We should help with dinner too," Eva said. She didn't want to walk away from Miles. She hurt from watching them thump each other for so long.

As she walked away, she heard Clint say, "You think Lily is just going to keep waiting around her entire life?"

Her spine straightened, and she strained to hear Miles's answer.

As far as she could tell, he didn't respond.

The fight was about Lily, then. Did Clint like the lady too?

Eva had no answers. Should she just ask?

Glancing back, she saw Miles standing in the ring, watching her go. His headgear was off, his hands half unwrapped. His hair was tousled and his face battered. He looked like the image of a perfect hero in her mind. She couldn't be imagining the yearning in his eyes.

No matter how drawn she was to Miles, she felt worse for Lily with every passing moment. The lady had waited faithfully for Miles, the most incredible military hero, to come home. She had probably prayed for his safety, knowing he was loyal to her but had to serve his country because of the faithful type of man he was.

Until the famous actress got attacked and the military hero almost kissed her and looked longingly at her.

Eva had stolen Miles's attention from Lily. She wanted no part of that.

Why, then, couldn't she glance away from Miles's blue gaze?

CHAPTER
Twelve

MILES WAS ANNOYED WITH CLINT, with himself, with Lily even. It was true he'd let her wait too long, not manning up and ending the relationship, but she was the one who turned the question around and asked him if he wanted to date other people. She always seemed relieved when he'd replied no. Her crying when he'd tried to break up six months ago still baffled him. It was so unlike her it had thrown him for a loop.

The sparring match with him and Clint had him sore and had solved nothing, but it felt great to get that much steam out. Especially with how pent-up he was, wanting to be with Eva and owing it to Lily to talk to her first.

He made it through dinner with Clint getting surlier by the moment, Easton and Walker teasing Eva, Mama and Papa laughing at their boys but giving Clint and Miles worried looks. Mama rarely stopped them from fighting anymore, but that didn't mean she liked it.

After dinner, they all pitched in to clean up while Papa took

Mama on a walk. The tension in his chest and between him and Clint was growing. Clint flirted with Eva like Walker and Easton, but he acted like Lily was *his* responsibility or long-lost love. That made little sense as he'd dated Sheryl for a year and had been engaged and almost married the two-faced Sheryl six months ago.

Miles couldn't even figure out his own life, so he didn't try to riddle out Clint's. He had to deal with the boulder sitting on his chest or he would implode. Eva asked Walker and Easton if she could help with their nighttime chores, and they both readily agreed. She ran upstairs to change out of her dress. Miles made sure he was waiting outside her bedroom door as she came out, looking fabulous in jeans and a T-shirt.

"Oh." She stopped and peered up at him. "Is the nose all right?"

He tested it and winced. "Not broken."

"Good." She moved to walk around him. "I'm going with Walker and Easton. They'll make sure I'm safe."

"I know." He put a hand on her arm. She stopped. "Eva … I don't know how to explain to you without sounding like a world-class idiot. I need to take care of some things and then I'm hoping we could talk …" He scrubbed at his beard. He *did* sound like a world-class idiot.

"Don't worry about me," Eva said, all bright and fake. "Walker and Easton will take good care of me."

He could bet his brothers would. He didn't want to leave her alone with any of them, but he had to talk everything out with Lily, make a clean break once and for all. If heaven had any favors for him, Eva would listen to him and give him a chance.

"That's true," he managed. "Can we talk … after?"

"No." She shook her head. "There's no need for us to talk.

From what I understand, you have someone loyal to you. You should focus on her."

She whirled and rushed across the upstairs hall and down the stairs.

Miles let out a heavy breath and let her go. What else was he supposed to do? Would she listen when he tried to explain? He doubted it.

He texted Lily, determined to see this through.

I'm in Coleville. Can you meet me?

Her response was immediate.

I didn't know you were coming home.

It was a surprise to me too. He tapped out the words and waited a long minute, pacing the upstairs hall.

I'm just getting off a shift at the hospital. I could meet you at the dock.

He didn't want to meet at the lake. A place they used to kiss when they were teenagers. It didn't matter, though. This wasn't going to be one of those meetings. He also didn't want to go face her family. He loved the Lillywhites. They'd always treated him like one of their own. Would everybody hate him after tonight? Probably. His own mama wasn't going to be happy. She'd long been planning the wedding with her friend Ivy, Lily's mom. But this was so past due he couldn't stand delaying any longer.

See you there.

He hurried through the house, grabbing his hat from the laundry room and realizing he hadn't even asked one of his brothers to borrow their truck. He'd text Walker. Walker wouldn't care. He stomped out of the house and around front. Clint stood there, his hat on his head. He wasn't even reclining against his truck as he waited. Another fist fight?

"I don't like fighting with you," Clint said.

"Really? I love fighting you." He meant it. Clint was as good a match to spar with as anyone he regularly duked it out with.

Clint smiled. "Okay, I like the fight. I don't like the feeling of us being at odds. Cade and I fought, emotionally, for over a year about Sheryl. It was an ugly feeling in my gut all the time. I don't want that with you."

"Maybe you do like the emotional fighting. You're the one who keeps being all tense and taking shots at me," Miles challenged, plunking his hat on his head to shield his eyes from the setting sun and folding his arms across his chest. He wasn't one to start a fight, but he wouldn't back down from someone coming at him.

"I'm ticked at the way you're treating Lily." Clint rubbed at the back of his neck and peered at him under his hat. "She's an angel and deserves better and you're the most loyal person I know. What gives? You meet the famous actress that Easton and Walker have always crushed on and you start two-timing Lily? That's not the straight-arrow, loyal brother I remember."

Miles flared instantly, but he could see Clint's point of view. Clint wasn't as easy to confide in as Walker or Easton, so he didn't even know about the many times Miles had tried to set Lily free. Of course no one would believe how unique and special Eva was. Not simply some 'famous actress'. Not to him.

"Lily and I were a fun senior year of high school romance," he said slowly. "When I first went into the Navy, it was nice having someone beautiful and fun to text or FaceTime with, get packages from, a photo to make my buddies envious, someone to hang out with and kiss when I came home."

Clint listened, but his fists grew tighter. "So you used Lily to have a girl back home?"

He was right. That was what Lily had become to Miles. The

girl back home, not the woman he loved or his future wife or anything close to the level of commitment he displayed toward her. He imagined it was the same for her; she could brag about her military boyfriend. Maybe she needed that to keep other men at a distance. Who knew?

"It wasn't a couple of years and the novelty wore off. I did love Lily, but it became more a good friend than anything romantic. Our calls got shorter and less frequent, and I rarely gave her anything more than a quick peck and hug when I visited."

"Why have you strung her along, then?" Clint demanded.

Miles blew out a breath. "I've tried, many times, to tell her to date and give other guys a chance." Clint's gaze was shielded by the hat and the dying sun. He couldn't get a bead on what his brother was thinking. "Every time she's asked if I wanted to date someone else and the honest answer was no. I was focused on the SEALs, not in places to meet women or date." He shrugged. "Then you know how it is with Mama and Ivy planning the wedding already."

Clint actually smiled. "Planning the wedding is an understatement. Ivy Lillywhite has had your tux and boutonniere picked out for years."

Miles smiled too. He loved Lily's mom and family. It was another reason this was so hard. He continued, "Six months ago, I knew I had to end it. It was past time."

"Six months ago?"

"I had a few weeks' leave for your wedding."

"I remember." Clint's voice went hard.

"I tried once again to end it with Lily. She sobbed and clung to me. Seeing Lily cry like that ripped me up inside. She's not the type to fake tears."

"That's for sure. She's the type to comfort anyone else who's crying and selfishly forget about herself."

"I know." Miles again wondered what Clint was feeling. "Anyway, I felt awful, I held her while she cried and then we parted ways without resolving anything."

Clint peered at him. He stepped closer and tilted his hat back. Miles could see the Coleville blues. They had a bit of sympathy in them now. "You haven't been promising you'd retire from the SEALs and come home and marry her? That's supposedly why she never moved to California to be near you."

"What? I'm not retiring, and neither of us has ever talked about her moving there. Who told you that?"

He grimaced. "Sheryl."

"You're still talking to Sheryl?"

"No. Six months ago, a couple days before she ditched me, she told me that when you came home for the wedding."

"And you believed her? With all the other lies she told you and Cade?" Miles shook his head in disgust.

"You have a valid point." Clint lifted his hands. He didn't know humble. "I'm pretty messed up where Sheryl Dracon is concerned."

"I can see that. Do you need some counseling or something, man?"

Clint bristled. "I don't know what kind of mumbo jumbo is happening in Southern Cali, but here in Montana, real men don't get counseling."

"Oh, boy." Miles rolled his eyes. He'd worked with a therapist after losing close friends in the military and following some of the horrific missions he'd been a part of. It had helped. "Yeah, that makes you really manly. Never deal with your issues so everybody around you can suffer. That's exactly the kind of example Papa would want you to be."

"Whatever. This isn't about me." Clint closed down quick. "So now that you've met the woman of your dreams, Eva Chevron, coincidentally the woman of every guy's fantasies, you're going to finally make the clean break with Lily so you can pursue Eva."

"I have to make the clean break with Lily. It's the right thing to do, even if it's late. Whether I ever have a chance with Eva…" He shook his head. "That remains to be seen. I ticked her off after I rescued her and she almost kissed me and I told her I had a girl back home." He didn't repeat what she'd just said about focusing on the person who was loyal to him.

"Ouch." Clint winced. "Makes sense why she's conflicted about you. She's definitely drawn to you, though. Anyone can see that, feel the 'sparks' between you, as Mama would say."

"I feel them," Miles admitted, not laughing at his tough big brother saying 'sparks'. It was out of character. "After meeting Eva …" He shook his head, trying to think how to explain to a man who didn't feel emotion. "I barely know her, but the way I'm drawn to her, the way she makes me sizzle with one look or touch. That's what I want. She's what I want." He took his hat off and hit the brim. "Do you really think I have a chance with Eva Chevron?"

"Do you even see yourself? Women go insane over the humble Navy SEAL and cowboy hero combination."

Miles shook his head. He didn't care about that. "They go insane over you as well."

"What does that matter if it's not the right one?" Clint challenged.

"Who *is* your right one?" Miles threw back at him, praying

he wouldn't say Sheryl Dracon. That 'dragon witch' as Easton called her better never return.

"That's not the subject tonight."

"Is it ever going to be?"

"Doubtful. Back to you. If you're wondering if you have a chance with the one and only famous actress Eva Chevron, the answer is probably no."

"Ouch. Sugarcoat if for me, please." Miles's heart thudded dully in his chest.

"But if you care for Eva, the sweet, funny, trusting, brave, and talented lady you're protecting, that's a different story. If you're interested in the real Eva, I think you two might have a chance. If you're only after the famous Eva Chevron persona, you don't deserve the real Eva."

He'd had the exact same thoughts. "You're right. I was enamored with Eva Chevron, as I imagine most men are, but meeting the real Eva, seeing how resiliently and bravely she dealt with being attacked, escaping with me, having to trust somebody she didn't know, laughing and talking with her, the brief times we've touched, the way she smiles and looks at me. That blows Eva Chevron, and any other woman in the world, out of the water."

"Good." Clint stepped up and clapped him on the shoulder. "Sorry about your nose. I think it's broken."

Miles touched it. "Nah. I've broken it before. This isn't too bad."

"Good luck talking to Lily. Be gentle with her."

"You know I will." There was something in his brother's eyes. Was Lily the woman Clint was interested in? He thought Walker had it bad for Lily, but maybe it was Clint who would pursue her. "If you're interested in Lily, I am even more sorry that this has dragged on for so long."

"No way." Clint put up his hands and backed up. "I'm not. No. It's a horse trough full of no for me."

"You're sure?" He was protesting a bit too much.

"See you tomorrow." Clint strode to his truck and was roaring out of the driveway before Miles could tap out the text asking Walker to borrow his truck. He got a thumbs-up back almost immediately.

He debated what to say to Lily as he drove toward the large lake near town where everyone boated in the summertime and ice skated or played hockey in the winter, but his mind kept spinning to what he'd say to Eva. He wanted to simply kiss her for a long time first, get out some of the withheld emotion he felt about her, and then talk through everything. The sparring match with Clint had probably gone on for over forty minutes and still he needed to release more tension.

Lily waited, standing on the dock in the shadows. The lights from the parking lot didn't quite reach her. When he stepped on to the wood, she hurried toward him.

"Miles!" She threw her arms around his neck and hugged him. She was a beautiful and fit lady, an accomplished nurse, and her family ran a charitable ranch for those displaced from their homes due to one reason or another.

Lily was an example of Christian light, hard work, and loyalty. There was not a thing wrong with her. She simply wasn't his right fit. He'd known it for a while. It was time to help her see the truth she'd been denying for some reason.

He hugged her briefly and then stepped away.

"You look fabulous," she said. "It's been too long."

"Yeah. You look great too."

"Why are you home?"

"Helping out a friend," he said. "Lily, listen. We've got to talk about something serious." He should maybe take her hand, but that might make it harder, and he only wanted to hold Eva's hand.

She looked up at him, smiling as if the something serious was a good thing. Nothing to do but plunge through this.

"Six months ago, I tried to break it off between us, and you cried and … I had no idea what to do."

Her smile faltered. "Before Clint's wedding day."

He nodded and rubbed at his jaw. It was interesting that Clint's wedding was her point of reference, but that wasn't the subject tonight. "I never want to make you cry again, but Lily … it's over. It has to be over."

"What's over?" she asked cautiously, though her eyes revealed she knew what he was saying.

"You and me. Our relationship. It's done."

"Why?" Lily backed up, her face pinched.

"You were one of my best friends, Lily, but we've grown apart over the years. If there were romantic feelings as teenagers, they're long gone now."

"That's just because we don't see each other," she protested.

He knew that wasn't the issue. Not after the 'sparks' he'd felt with Eva from one look or touch. "I'm not moving back here, and you've never even brought up the subject of moving to California," he said instead.

"I could," she said, but he could tell she didn't want to. She'd never wanted to, and that was fine.

"Your family is here. You love your work, you love all the children on your ranch, and you love Montana. I get it, Lily. Our relationship is not enough of a draw for you to relocate."

"That's not fair," she said.

"It's not, and I'm not putting this on you. I should've set you free years ago."

She blinked at him. Her lip wobbled, and he felt like the biggest of jerks.

"Lily ... can you honestly say that you love me desperately and you hate every day we're apart? Can you say that you light up when I look at you or touch you, and you'd elope tomorrow if I could make it work?" These thoughts were all churning in him as he realized he hated each second away from Eva, and she lit him up with one glance or brush of her fingers.

Lily stared at him. Tears rolled down her smooth cheeks and made her eyes even brighter.

Not tears. Not again.

Miles prayed he could make her see they weren't a right fit without hurting her.

"I can't do this," she murmured, turning away from him and brushing angrily at her tears.

He had no clue how to respond.

Apparently not hurting Lily wouldn't be possible.

He couldn't abort the mission, but he prayed it wouldn't be a failure. Somehow, he had to get through to her.

CHAPTER Thirteen

EVA HELPED Easton and Walker with chores. When they got back to the house and Miles still wasn't home, she wanted to just take a shower and go to bed, not think about him being with Lily, holding her hand, cuddling her, kissing her. Her stomach turned over, and she feared she'd puke.

Easton and Walker didn't let her wallow. They let her shower and change into a T-shirt and shorts, but then they made popcorn, compiled drinks and treats, and started the movie *A-Team* in the theater down the hall from Eva's bedroom. Easton promised the show was 'gas', even if she wasn't starring in it. His teenage lingo was funny.

Eva liked the action and witty dialogue in the movie. She knew a couple of the actors personally but still had to pretend to be invested. She was miserable inside. Miles was with Lily. If Eva cared about Miles and his happiness, and had felt bad for Lily, she should be happy for both of them. He was finally with his girl back home. She selfishly wished he'd choose her. That was messed up. Lily had been loyal to him for how many years? It sounded like a lot. Now Miles was seeing her again, holding her, kissing her.

Eva flinched and stood quickly.

"You all right?" Easton asked.

"I need to use the bathroom," she said, rushing out of the theater into the hallway and pumping down the stairs. She pushed down the handle on the front door, shoved it open, and ran out onto the front porch. Pausing by the railing, she drew in some breaths of fresh air. If only she could go on a long walk in the crisp night air. She knew this ranch was safe, but they were all still diligent with her protection, and she didn't want to stress anyone if she took off.

"Eva," Walker called, and she heard his footsteps on the stairs.

Lights flashed through the trees and the rumble of a truck approached. Eva backed up as Walker reached her. He steadied her with his hand on her arm.

"You all right?"

Walker noticed the headlights before she could respond. He stepped in front of her to shield her and ushered her back into the foyer. His body was coiled, the muscles in his arms flexing, one palm resting on his sidearm.

Then he relaxed. "It's my truck. It's Miles."

Eva did the opposite of relaxing. Her body filled with warmth and longing. Miles was back. Had he come for her? She edged around Walker, anxious to see him. Then disgust at her own reaction filled her. He'd been with Lily for over two hours. She was certain of it. She had never fallen prey to the loose guidelines about relationships that seemed to prevail in her industry. She wouldn't be the other woman. Why was she letting down her guard now?

The truck stopped, the engine cut, and Miles hopped out. The front porch lights revealed his handsome face shadowed by the cowboy hat. His strong form outlined in a T-shirt, jeans, cowboy boots, and hat. Her body filled with warmth. He was irresistible. It wasn't just his good looks. She was drawn to him, body and soul.

"Eva," he said so softly she barely heard it.

Butterflies filled her stomach, and her breathing shortened.

Miles strode across the driveway and to the porch. A man on a mission.

Eva's feet betrayed her, and she rushed to meet him.

Miles pounded up the steps, determination in the lines of his face and body, anticipation in his blue eyes.

He stopped on the top step. She was at the edge of the porch. They were close to the same height, and the look of longing he gifted her with set her heart racing.

"Eva." He said her name reverently. "There's so much I have to tell you. I …"

Then he wrapped his arms around her, and she willingly went into his arms. He held her tight to his chest. Every wrong was made right. Being in Miles's arms was her spot. She owned this spot and never wanted to leave it.

The door closed behind them. Eva turned to look, but the porch was empty. Walker had stepped back into the house to give them privacy.

She looked back around at Miles. Being in his arms thrilled her. What would he tell her? Could she believe him? Trust him? She hadn't trusted a man in years. Even with how confused she was about him and their relationship, if they even had one, she knew Miles was honest.

She waited for all those things he had to tell her, but his gaze dropped to her lips, and he breathed out, "I've known you for twenty-four hours, Eva, and I feel like I've been resisting kissing you for several lifetimes."

Eva had heard every line in the book. She cherished this one. It was better than anything she'd heard on the set or off. Was it just a line or did he mean it? Even an honest cowboy could drop a schmoozy line to try to get a famous actress to kiss him.

In Miles's arms, it was impossible to think straight or to believe he wasn't genuine. She believed she was the deepest yearning of his heart. His touch was magical, and she was consumed by him.

He tilted his head, fused their mouths together, and captured her completely.

Captured was too mild. Miles Coleville took command of her lips like a man on a mission, a soldier returning from war and kissing his lifelong love, a cowboy claiming his girl with all the determination, thoroughness, and loyalty a cowboy could display, a man aching for the woman he'd loved his entire life and finally they were melded together. They were one heart, body, and soul.

The description was too much, yet it didn't feel like nearly enough.

Eva wrapped her arms around his neck and returned the kiss. She knocked off his hat and mussed up his thick hair. She knew he didn't care about the hat. He didn't care about anything but her.

The front door opened and then quickly closed again. They ignored it.

Miles swept her off her feet, carried her across the porch and to the swing. He settled into the wide seat with her cradled as close as she could be to his strong chest. She could feel his heart pounding against hers as the swing rocked and then settled.

He paused for half a beat, threaded his hand into her hair, massaging her scalp and making her tingle head to toe. Then he whispered, "Oh, Eva," before he kissed her again.

They exchanged kisses born of desperation, longing, love. They were conquering the fear together that they would never get here, never be together. Reaching this spot, entangled in Miles's arms, him securing her heart, she knew it was worth the long, long wait. Several lifetimes, just as he'd said.

They exchanged kisses created of and fueling the sparks between them that no longer had to be denied. Forbidden love no more. Their love could soar as they became one. The passion and joy of their being together grew until Eva suspected the sun was rising again, bursting over the mountains, lifted and fueled by their joy and their perfect kisses.

The kisses slowed down, and she clung to him. She felt blessedly content and crazily in love. She was drugged by Miles—his lips, his nearness, his strength, the fact that his kisses were unparalleled, never to be equaled, except by him. Each day, there would be new kisses to explore and savor. They could kiss until the sun rose and set. They could kiss until Aiden solved all her dark web issues. They could kiss until he had to leave on a SEAL assignment or she had to go on location for a movie. Being apart would be a torture all its own, but it would make moments like this even more incredible. The future was wide open for them.

Miles pulled back just enough to meet her gaze. "Eva ..." He studied her. "That was incredible. You are incredible. I feel like … I've been hiding so much—"

Hiding? She didn't like the sound of that.

The front door flung open, banging against the house. Mama came storming out. Eva buried her head in Miles's neck, embarrassed that his mother had caught them kissing and cuddling. She took a long inhale of his manly scent. He didn't smell like his delicious and mind-clouding bergamot and pineapple. He smelled sweet, like flowers, a uniquely feminine scent. What flower was it …

Eva pulled back to look at him, but she didn't get the chance to say anything.

"Miles Coleville, I would like to speak to you about Lily," Mama said. She looked as angry as when Autumn had propositioned Easton.

Lilies. Miles smelled like lilies.

Mama should be angry. Furious, in fact. Eva was making out with her son, who was dating someone else. Eva should be angry too. At herself. At him. Hiding? He was hiding a girlfriend who smelled like the flower she was named after.

Eva yanked out of his arms and scrambled to her feet. He'd been with Lily, close enough he smelled like her.

The off-the-chart kisses she and Miles had exchanged were instantly tainted with the stink of betrayal.

She glared at him and seethed, "I am not into two-timers."

Mama folded her arms and glared at Miles as well.

Miles stood, holding his hands out. "Eva, it's not like that. I broke up with Lily tonight."

"Because you want to be with me?" she asked, her stomach churning.

"Yes." He nodded, stepping closer. "It's you for me, Eva. You have to see that."

"And give up on thirteen years with Lily?" his mother interjected. "That poor girl worships you and needs you."

Eva was nauseated. Thirteen years? Poor girl was right. She'd been cheated on herself. It was horrific. She'd seen this scene play out at movie sets, men and women getting together and betraying their significant other waiting back home. Sickening. She had never been part of the disgusting hookups. Ever. She'd let down her guard because she thought Miles was special, that they were special.

"You would break up a thirteen-year relationship over someone you met last night?" Eva shook her head, bile rising in her throat. "You don't even know me. You only think we have something special because I'm famous." Whirling away, she darted around Mama and for the front door.

"Eva, that's not true," Miles called after her.

He moved to go around Mama, but his mother grabbed his arm and hissed, "I cannot believe you would—"

Eva made it inside. She ran past Walker, Jared, and Easton, who all stood in the foyer looking at her. She couldn't look at any of them.

She was on the third stair when Walker's voice stopped her. "Eva, my brother wouldn't—"

She cried out and put her hands over her ears. "Please don't." Racing up the stairs, she made it into her room and slammed the door, pushing the lock button. She hurried into the bathroom and shut that door and locked it as well.

How could Miles do that to her? To Lily?

Tears trailed down her face. She touched her lips, unwittingly reliving the most incredible kisses she'd ever received in her life. She'd been swept away like magic in a Disney movie. But that wasn't real. She knew that.

Had he kissed Lily like that earlier tonight? Before he broke up with his lifelong girlfriend so he could be with Eva Chevron, the famous actress. Was it her insecurities acting up, or was a relationship with Miles doomed just like every other relationship she'd ever tried?

"Argh!" she screamed. She sank to the tile floor, her back against the door, and put her head between her hands. The tears came more freely.

For the past twenty-four hours, she felt like she'd found the man she'd always longed for.

And he would dump a thirteen-year relationship to his loyal girlfriend for someone he didn't even know. Why? Because he was infatuated with Eva because she was famous and he *thought* he knew her?

That felt wrong for the Miles she knew, but she'd seen it so many times she couldn't deny it was probably the reason. She had believed they had a bond that was unparalleled, but she didn't know what to think now. All she'd known up to this point was Lily was the 'girl back home', which could mean any manner of things. But the way his family reacted to him breaking up with Lily, and thirteen years together? Thirteen years of Lily waiting faithfully for him? This was much more serious than Eva had understood.

Eva felt awful for herself, losing the dream of Miles.

She felt more awful for Lily.

Miles Coleville was a deceitful playboy. She would never have believed it. Somehow, she had to wrap her mind around it and digest it.

She could only pray Aiden's team would solve her other

dilemma. She had no idea how she'd last another day around her bodyguard.

CHAPTER
Fourteen

MILES STAYED on the porch and talked through everything with his parents, repeating a lot of what he'd told Clint earlier and going over the details of his relationship with Lily. He explained he and Lily had agreed tonight that they were done and they hadn't had a real relationship in years.

He and Lily had sat on the dock talking for a long time. She'd admitted there was someone she had fallen for, but she was adamant they couldn't be together. She refused to give him a name. He guessed it could be Clint or Walker but wasn't about to pry. His brothers were man enough to step up and pursue her if it was right.

She told him part of the reason she broke down six months ago was in regards to that man, but another reason was a 'bad situation'. She wouldn't give him any details about the situation and let him go 'renegade' on her. Having a Navy SEAL boyfriend had protected her throughout school and at the hospital. When Miles had said he didn't want to date anyone else every time they talked about it, she'd been relieved to keep up the status quo.

Lily agreed it was past time they were done 'pretending to be a couple' in her words. He was relieved he wasn't breaking her heart or anything, but he wanted her to give him more details about the bad situation and let him help. Lily was more strong-willed than even he remembered and she said she would figure it out. He finally extracted her promise that if she was in danger, she'd let Clint know. She acted really off about that, and it made him wonder more than ever if she had feelings for Clint.

There wasn't much he could share with his parents as he'd promised Lily, so the questions went round and round and his mama got more frustrated with him by the moment. He normally wouldn't feel so impatient about it. He enjoyed discussing things with his parents and getting their advice during the rare times he was home.

But Eva had stormed off, thought he was a two-timer, thought he only wanted her because she was famous. He had to get to her, talk this through, and pray she'd listen and give him a chance to prove how loyal he could be. Had those out of this world kisses not affected her at all? He knew that he and Eva had something much more substantial than a physical relationship, but those kisses consumed him.

Mama finally calmed down and his parents both conceded that he was right, he and Lily weren't a fit and Lily should date and move on. They exchanged a look after the words 'move on' and he wondered if they'd both noticed Walker and possibly Clint's interest in Lily.

"You need to go patch things up with our Eva," Mama surprised him by saying.

"I want to," he admitted, edging toward the door.

"I like Eva. I just always thought you'd marry Lily. Ivy and I have been planning it for years."

"I know you have." He didn't tell her that was part of the pressure he'd felt. It was eye-opening that Lily had clung to the relationship for different reasons than he'd foreseen. He'd have to mention to Clint to keep an eye on her, even if he couldn't tell his brother why. That would bug Clint. It was bugging him.

"It'll take me a spell to wrap my mind around this." She pursed her lips. "If you marry Eva, you'll never move home, will you?"

"Oh, Mama." Miles chuckled and gave her a quick squeeze. "I'm not anywhere close to marrying anyone."

"Whyever not? You're thirty years old, son. I mean, my goodness sakes, what are you waiting for? Any of you boys could settle down and have a family tomorrow. Even Hudson is old enough. It's not as if doctors don't finish up residency with a spouse and sometimes children in tow. Does anyone around here care that I need grandbabies?"

"I care," his dad said, grinning at her.

"Don't you patronize me." Mama swatted at Papa and then she kissed him. It wasn't just a peck, either.

Miles took that as his cue to leave. He rushed through the front door, intent on getting to Eva and somehow explaining everything. Would she ever believe his intentions were true? That she was the right one for him and Lily never had been?

He feared the answer was no.

Easton and Walker were by the stairs.

"You okay?" Walker asked.

"No, it's a mess. But I broke up with Lily and she ... had some different reasons for staying together so long."

"Such as?"

"Her secrets to share."

Walker didn't appear to like that but he wouldn't pry. "Where is she?"

"Home, I'd assume."

"Do you think it's too late?" He looked at Easton.

"Yes. Calm down, bro. Give the lady a minute to restructure her future plans from being centered on 'devastatingly handsome Lieutenant Miles Coleville' before you go chasing after her. You don't want to be the rebound guy."

Miles needed to get to Eva, but he couldn't quite compute that Easton was the one who'd just said that piece of advice. "Did you just …"

Easton shrugged. "I listen to some of the lectures, okay?"

Miles smiled. He sobered as he glanced at Walker. "Keep an eye on her."

Walker's eyes widened. "Tonight?"

"No. I'm saying in general. She's an independent lady but she might need some help."

Walker's head bobbed. He rubbed at his jaw line and looked at the front door like he wanted to make a run for it.

"Come on, bro." Easton grabbed his arm. "Let's go spar for a bit so you can calm down."

Miles hurried up the stairs. Lily had admitted there was someone else, and it appeared Walker and maybe Clint were interested in her. That could get messy. Who was he to say who should be with who? He sure hoped Walker didn't get his heart broken.

Reaching the end of the hall, he stopped. His fist raised to pound on the door, but he stayed it and was able to rap somewhat softly. He waited. No noise inside the room.

"Eva?" he called.

He knocked again. Waited. Had she come into her room? As her bodyguard, he had to make certain. He pulled out his phone and called Easton. "You saw Eva go up the stairs and to her room?"

"Just up the stairs, but I heard two doors open and close, so I assumed she went into her bedroom and then her bathroom."

"Thanks." He pocketed his phone, knocked again and heard nothing. He quickly checked the other upstairs rooms. Empty. His chest tightened. They'd all relaxed because of the drama with him, Lily, and Eva. More than likely, Eva just wasn't answering because she was upset at him, but if there was any chance of danger …

Returning to Eva's door, he knocked louder and then called, "Eva. I need to know you're safe. If you don't open the door, I'm coming in to check."

He waited with bated breath. What if she wasn't safe? They'd had no alerts, nobody getting through the gate, but something crazy could've happened—a person hiding under the frame of a truck or somehow finding a vulnerable spot where they could maneuver over the fence, disabling the cameras, sneaking into the house …

Footsteps approached from inside the bedroom and the door cracked, but not enough to see her beautiful face. He longed to just see her, see for himself that she was all right, that she didn't hate him and think he was some two-timer. He thought he should deserve some credit for not kissing her until he broke it off completely with Lily. It had been a struggle, that was for sure.

"I'm fine," she muttered through the crack.

"I'm glad," he said softly. "I need to see you to make certain you are safe."

"Fine," she snarled, flinging the door open. She looked upset, vulnerable, and in need of him holding her close. Holding her arms out wide, she shot at him, "All in one piece and no bad guys hiding in my room."

"I had to make sure."

She nodded and dropped her arms, apparently reading him and knowing he wanted to step in and wrap his arms around her.

"Can we talk?" he asked.

"No."

"Later?"

"Goodnight, Miles." She shut the door.

Miles stared at the closed door for far too long. She'd shut him out. Out of her heart.

He'd feared when he finally was able to do the honorable thing and break up with Lily face to face, he would have lost his chance with Eva.

Turns out, his fears were more than grounded.

Miles woke early the next morning and went to lift weights. He was back and showered before any movement came from the room next door. He took to pacing in front of the door. He hadn't slept well and had spent most of the night analyzing what he could've done differently, what he could do to fix things now, and praying for some kind of insight because he had none.

His phone buzzed on his hip. He pulled it out. Aiden.

"Hey."

"Autumn was attacked early this morning."

"What?" Miles stopped pacing and leaned against the wall, clinging to the phone.

"Yeah. Good old Agent Ryken Henderson let himself in, went right into the bedroom, and when he realized she wasn't Eva, he went ballistic."

The door opened slowly behind him. He spun. Eva stood there in a white sundress, her expression guarded. There must've been something in his face because immediately her eyes widened in concern. "What's going on?"

"Aiden. Eva is here. I'm putting the phone on speaker."

Eva edged up close to him, her coconut scent washing over him.

"Eva. Ryken attacked Autumn this morning in your bedroom."

"No!" Eva cried out, swaying on her feet.

Miles wasted no time shifting the phone to his left hand and wrapping his right arm around Eva's waist, pulling her into his side. He couldn't let himself get distracted by how perfectly she fit against him.

"Is she all right?" Eva asked.

"Of course she's all right. She's Autumn Cardon. Even with the jump on her and surprising her out of a sound sleep, a loser like Agent Henderson couldn't defeat Autumn. A few bruises and scrapes and you might need to redecorate your bedroom. She broke a few knickknacks on his skull."

"Oh, thank heavens she's all right." Eva relaxed into Miles.

Miles relaxed too. Autumn wasn't seriously hurt, Henderson would be arrested, and Eva was cuddled against his side. Maybe all his prayers would be answered.

"I spoke with Agent Henderson at length," Aiden continued. "He placed all the blame on Jorge Augilar. We finally found a money trail from Jorge's uncle to Henderson. Apparently Henderson and Jorge had an agreement for Henderson to gain your trust and then abduct you, get you across the border. When Henderson failed the other night, Jorge changed the plan and had an associate put all the hits up on the dark web. Jorge is on lockdown and the requests have been removed from the dark web. We're still not sure who was going to help Jorge escape. Hopefully we'll find them."

Aiden paused. Eva looked up at Miles. There was longing and frustration in her eyes.

"So it's over?" Eva asked.

"It's over," Aiden agreed. "Paul's on his way to retrieve you both. Miles, you can finish your long weekend in my beautiful home. Eva, I am having my people install better security for you. I'd recommend you hire some of my guards, or move to a gated community with guards, but I can't force you to do that."

"I'll think about it."

"That's all we can ask. It's been a pleasure, Eva. Grateful we could be of service."

"Thank you," she said. "Please bill me."

Aiden chuckled. "I'm sure some of my people will take payment, but I don't know about Lieutenant Coleville. You two will have to figure things out. Talk soon." He hung up.

Eva straightened away from Miles and hurried back into the door of her room. She turned to face him. Miles thought that was the opposite of Aiden's advice to 'figure things out'.

"Well, that's wonderful. It's over." She had a bright, fake smile on her face.

Why those words were a punch to the gut Miles wasn't certain. She meant the hits on the web, the Agent Henderson and Jorge Augilar mess being over. He was sixty percent certain that was what she meant.

"I'll go get ready to fly home."

She shut the door before he could ask if he could extend the conversation—see how she was feeling about her situation, see how she was feeling about the two of them. At the moment, there wasn't a *them*.

Miles felt his shoulders round as he hurried to throw his stuff into his duffel bag and then waited for her to come out. He waited and waited. Far too much time to stew about everything. Eva was safe. That was most important. They were a mess and most likely he had no hope of a future with her. That was horrific.

Finally, the door opened. She didn't look at him. Her eyes were red-rimmed. She was wearing a white T-shirt and pink joggers.

She lifted the suitcase from Autumn out of the room. Miles hurried to take it from her.

"Thank you." She brushed past him.

"Eva, please," he said to her back.

She paused but didn't look back.

"Can we talk about this?"

"I'm sure we'll have too much time to talk on the plane." She still didn't look at him as she hurried downstairs.

Miles hefted his duffel bag and followed, leaving her suitcase and his bag by the front door. They ate breakfast with the family. Eva chatted brightly with everyone, said her thank yous and her goodbyes. Mama hugged her tightly and Miles heard a murmured, "Give my boy a chance."

Eva stiffened and pulled back. "Thank you, Mama. I hope to

see all of you again. If you're ever in California, please let me know." She turned and strode out of the kitchen.

Miles gave Mama a helpless shrug, grateful she'd tried, but nothing seemed to be getting through to Eva. He'd seen first-hand how brave and resilient she was. Now she was using those skills, and her acting expertise, to shut him out.

Walker drove them to Kalispell and the airport. Eva drew Walker out about roping, even though Miles could've sworn they'd already had this conversation. She told Walker about her dad's ranch and her two sisters, teasing that Walker should go meet her next-younger sister.

Miles stewed about how to convince her she was his perfect fit and see if she returned the feeling. He wanted the chance to talk for hours about everything and nothing.

They'd talk on the plane. He clung to that. Because if he didn't somehow talk this through with her on the plane, he might never see her again. He'd always planned on his future being his military career. Without Eva, he felt like his future was gaping and empty.

Paul swooped down on an Airbus a few minutes after they got to the airport. How many jets did Aiden own? The man was such an enigma and yet made Miles feel like he was his close friend.

It was good to see the tall pilot. Eva gave Walker a hug goodbye and thanked him, then walked over to the jet. Paul lifted a hand to Walker and followed.

"Good luck, bro," Walker said.

"I'm afraid I'm gonna need it." He shook his brother's hand, clapping him on the shoulder. "Good luck to you. Are you going after Lily?"

"I intend to." He tilted down his hat, hiding his expression.

"We'll see how it goes. Might be awkward trading one Coleville for another. She'll need some time for sure."

"I hope not. Hope I haven't messed everything up for you as well." He glanced back at Eva and saw her disappearing into the plane.

"Life is messy sometimes," Walker said. "We'll all figure it out. If we're supposed to. Turn to Jesus and it'll work."

"I spent most of the night praying," Miles said.

"Good man. I'm proud of you, brother."

"I'm proud of you too. See you soon." Miles lifted a hand and turned away. He didn't know why he said 'see you soon'. He didn't make it home often.

Walking onto the plane, he saw Paul standing next to Eva. Paul nodded to him and closed the door while Eva sank into a leather recliner.

Miles walked over and settled into the recliner next to hers. She didn't say anything, didn't even look at him, putting earbuds in and fiddling with the screen that pulled out of the seat.

He prayed for help and waited until the plane lifted off. He only had a few hours.

"Eva, I …" He turned to look at her. Her head was lolled to the side. She still had the earbuds in, and she looked for all the world to be sleeping.

Some guys in his unit could fall asleep that fast, and Eva had been through a lot in a day and a half. She was also one of the most accomplished actresses around. Was she faking sleep?

It seemed the last thing she wanted to do was talk to him. What could he do to get through to her? Had he messed this up so completely that he had no chance at all?

He studied her and kept praying.

CHAPTER
Fifteen

EVA SUFFERED THROUGH THE MINUTES, not even distracted by the movie playing on the screen and through her earbuds. She couldn't even tell what the movie was and keeping her eyes shut didn't help. She tried to breathe slow and easy. She could feel Miles's gaze on her.

They movie finished and she thought they had to be getting close to home.

She could keep her distance with Paul in the car, say thank you and goodbye, and never see Miles Coleville again. Her gut stirred with longing, and she had to focus on her 'sleeping' pose. She was an actress. She'd held odder-looking and more uncomfortable positions for a lot longer than this, but she hadn't been an emotionally overwrought mess.

She should probably give Miles a chance to say his piece, but she couldn't do it. A spell-binding look from those blue eyes, a touch from his magical fingers, and she'd fall into his enchantment. He'd make her feel special, he'd light her up with his kisses, and he might even pretend to love her until he met someone more famous.

She could see it now. Miles would look exceptional in his suit and she'd be on his arm, feeling like she was special and Miles was head over heels in love with her. They'd be at an exclusive party she usually hated going to by herself, but with Miles, she'd be happy to go anywhere. Then he'd notice somebody—a beautiful actress, influencer, or politician. Bermuda Venus or Jezebel Noir. Those two would drool over a real man like Miles, a military hero, a tough cowboy. Miles was too classy to act on their invitations with Eva right there on his arm, but before long, he'd move on, just like every guy she'd dated since she left home.

It was ironic that Miles could stay devoted to one woman for thirteen years and then suddenly shift his loyalties. Eva couldn't sort it out in her mind. She feared he'd been infatuated with her as a star and assumed that meant they had a connection.

What was her excuse, then? She knew they had a connection. It blew anything she'd experienced with any other man out of the water. His touch. The way his blue eyes mesmerized her. Those kisses. Enchanting. Out of this world.

She touched her fingers to her lips and sighed with longing.

Her earbud was removed. The movie she'd been pretending to sleep to had shut off a while ago.

"Eva." Miles's husky voice was too close to her ear. His unique bergamot and pineapple scent made her pulse speed up.

Opening her eyes and pivoting to get a bit of space and focus on him, she sighed louder. The bow in his upper lip, his intriguing blue eyes, the shadow of a beard on his firm jawline. Why did he have to appeal to her on every level?

"Have we been in the air long?" she asked brightly, pretending she had been asleep.

"Two and a half hours," he said, studying her. His blue eyes were wounded. Well, she was more wounded. He'd kissed her like the world was going to end minutes after kissing his girl. He'd dumped poor Lily because of Eva. That hurt too. She didn't want to be the cause of breaking up relationships. Everything hurt.

"Eva, will you listen to me?" His voice was patient and his eyes begged her to let him explain.

"Miles, it's ... whatever." She put up a hand to shield herself and thought she sounded like a valley girl. She took out her other earbud and set them aside, studiously avoiding looking at him. "We had a little fling. I'm over it."

She shifted in her seat and closed her eyes, praying for strength. Her acting skills weren't even helping. She couldn't go through the heartbreak again, and with Miles ... it would be a million times worse. She should hardly know him. Instead, she felt like he'd been created for her.

"A little fling?" Miles growled.

Her heart took off at the depth in his voice. She could not let herself look at him. This flight couldn't last much longer. They'd start to descend soon. She'd keep her distance until then.

Help me stay strong for half an hour more. Please, she begged heaven above.

"A little fling?" Miles repeated.

Eva squeezed her eyes shut. If she didn't say anything, she feared he'd do something drastic. What ... she had no idea. How drastic could you get on an airplane? He couldn't storm into her space, cup her jawline with those strong hands, promise her forever with one look from his blue eyes, eradicate any fears with his beguiling lips. Her heart raced out of control at the mere idea of kissing him again. The brave, humble, enticing Miles Coleville was irresistible to her.

She heard movement and her eyes popped open. She looked over. Miles was out of his seat and stepping up to hers. The determination in those blue eyes knocked the oxygen out of her lungs. He bent down and unbuckled her seatbelt, brushing her arm, her abdomen, her hip bone. Thankfully her shirt covered her abdomen and hip bone. They still tingled.

Her breath came in gulps and her skin prickled with anticipation. That look in his eyes. He was going to kiss her and kiss her and kiss her.

Miles slid his hands under her legs and her lower back and easily lifted her out of her seat.

"Miles!" She wrapped her arms around his neck. "What are you doing?" She tried to make her voice sound indignant, but it was breathy and yearning. If she could channel the way Miles made her feel for her next rom-com, she'd sell out theaters around the world. But this wasn't a movie. This was real. Far too real. It was exhilarating and incredible and it hurt. She couldn't pretend and put herself into a role. Not with Miles holding her close.

He didn't answer. His jaw was set, and a muscle popped in it. He turned and settled back into his seat with her cradled against his chest, perched on his lap, her arms around his neck. She released him, and her hands slid along his neck until they rested on his broad shoulders. She relished the feel of his well-developed muscles under her palms and fingertips.

His breath was coming quicker too. "A little fling?" he said for the third time. She wished she could tease him about it, but she couldn't get a breath to do anything but somehow get through the next few moments. "Does this feel like a little fling to you?"

"No," Eva admitted before she could stop herself.

"Eva." Her name came out as a groan. One of his hands stayed around her lower back and cradled her closer while the other came up to frame her jawline, his fingers threading into her hair.

Eva groaned too. She slid her hands along his shoulders and around to grasp his upper back and hold on. His lips angled toward hers, and heaven help her, she arched up to meet him.

The instant of connection was as powerful as their kisses last night. Magic. Another world. Eva couldn't think straight, couldn't worry about a thing. All she could do was respond to the pressure of his ravenous kiss and prove she was even more hungry for him.

His mouth lit up her world and his hands worked an enchantment of their own, making her feel safe and cherished and loved.

They kissed and kissed and she savored each movement, each exchange, each promise of love and devotion.

"Please buckle your seat belts for landing," Paul's voice said over the intercom, dry humor evident.

Eva startled and yanked away, gulping for oxygen.

Miles gave her a conspiratorial grin. "I'm afraid he has a camera up there to make certain all is well back here without a flight attendant on board."

"Oh!" Eva exclaimed, and then she broke from Miles's grasp and scrambled off his lap and into her own seat. She tried to buckle her seatbelt, but her fingers were trembling. Giving up on that, she touched her mouth with her fingertips and reveled in the memory of another series of award-winning kisses.

Miles chuckled softly, and before she knew it, he was leaning over and doing her seat belt up. His fingertips grazed her arm, her abdomen, and her hip again. She was on fire and only wanted to kiss him more.

He took her hand in his and raised it to his lips. Brushing his mouth against her knuckles and bringing tingles to her flesh, he murmured, "We'll have to continue this when I get you home and we're able to talk everything out." He gave her a meaningful look.

Eva was in desperate trouble. She'd let down her guard completely. Again. He could claim this wasn't a fling, but she knew how this went down. She almost ripped her hand free to try to clear her fogged-by-Miles brain, but that would be too telling.

She found herself clinging to his hand as the plane descended quickly. Miles rested their joined hands on his muscular thigh and traced patterns on the back of her hand with his thumb. He seemed comfortable and satisfied that he'd proven his point with his kisses. He'd proven something. If only she knew what. The brain fog from kissing him wasn't clearing.

Once she got home and forced herself to tell him goodbye, then she could think clearly. Then she could get back to her life.

A life without him. Misery. Her glamorous, busy, fulfilling, successful life was all fake, all fluff, no substance, no magical touches, no tingling kisses. She would be in sheer misery without Miles by her side.

She risked a glance at him. He smiled at her, his blue eyes shining with hope. She felt the same hope rise in her own heart.

What had she gotten herself into? How was she going to save her heart from breaking in two? She had to be strong. Better a preemptive strike and explaining to him that they had no future rather than falling any deeper for the mesmerizing cowboy and military man who could devastate her when he walked away.

But no matter if she ended it now or let him kiss her a few more dozen times. Going on without Miles would devastate her.

Could she justify kissing him a dozen times first?

That was selfish and the opposite of what either of them needed. She'd get home and then she'd end this fantasy with Miles. Hopefully he'd come to his senses and go back to his Lily.

Her heart thudded dully in her chest. How was she going to rip her own heart out?

CHAPTER
Sixteen

MILES WAS FLYING HIGH EVEN as the plane settled on the tarmac. He had Eva's hand in his and the memory of another unreal series of kisses on his lips. He was bursting with all the things he wanted to say to her, but he would wait until they were at her house and settled in. They could talk and talk for hours, then plan their future and kiss every spare minute.

He'd never been so lit up and ecstatic. Being with Eva was better than any successful mission, adventure thrill with parachute, surfboard, bike, or horse. He'd heard that quick relationships would burn out quick, but he felt just the opposite. His feelings for Lily had never been like this. He and Eva were just getting started. Their relationship was special, unique, and genuine. She was resilient and independent, the perfect fit for him. They would only build and soar from here.

They loaded up with Paul in an Escalade and he drove them to Eva's house, explaining more about what had happened with Autumn and Ryken, the police reports and what Eva would need to do to complete those, the security Aiden's people had installed, that Aiden would have someone watching over her until she hired her own security or signed a contract with him, and how Autumn was doing.

Was Eva growing more closed off the closer they got to her house? Was her smile too forced? What if she used her acting skills to hide what she really felt?

Doubts started tickling at his brain, but he couldn't give into them. He was getting a second chance with the only woman in the world for him. The way she'd kissed him and the way she was clinging to his hand and leaning into his shoulder told him she felt the same.

She'd been upset about him and Lily. Who wouldn't be? That was over and behind them. Lily was ready to be done and they both would be happier, as long as Lily was safe and turned to Clint if the situation she'd been using a 'Navy SEAL boyfriend' to keep her safe from got worse.

He and Eva could move through their pasts, share, and grow together. Eva would understand about Lily. Of course she would.

The tightness in his chest told him otherwise.

Paul walked them into the house. Two of Aiden's guards, Josh and Tyler, greeted them and shook their hands. They showed Eva the damage to her bedroom, which was actually pretty minimal: a vase, a hole in the wall, and a shattered mirror. They'd already cleaned it all up, except the hole that would need sheetrock and paint.

They explained how her new security system worked and sent the link to the cameras and sensors to her phone. They explained it would also be monitored at Aiden's security center at his main property in Long Island and one of them would be close by, staying in the VRBO that Paul had found and doing rotations every hour.

They thanked the men and Paul. Then Eva shut the door behind them. She didn't arm the alarm.

She turned to Miles, and she looked exhausted and concerned. Her deep-brown eyes had lost their sparkle.

"Hey." Miles gathered her close.

She clung to him, and her body trembled against his.

He held her for a few beats and she gradually relaxed, curling into him. Her head was in the crook of his neck, and he knew she was his perfect fit.

"You're worn out," he said. He was anxious to talk things out with her, but she'd been through a lot of stress and upheaval in a short time.

"I am," she admitted, looking up at him.

It was early afternoon. Did he dare suggest he stay here while she take a nap? Would that make her feel safer or push her boundaries? He'd been protecting her for only a day and a half, but he felt she was his to protect and care for. Going back to work on Tuesday would be rough. He'd never felt that way before. He'd lived for the hard work, camaraderie, and fulfillment of his Navy career.

"I can leave, let you get some rest." He chose his words carefully, watching her face. When she looked relieved, he didn't know how to take it. "I'll bring some takeout by later. We can eat and talk everything through." He waited, praying she wouldn't say no.

"Miles ..." She pressed a hand to her forehead. "I don't know that talking is going to accomplish anything."

"What do you mean?"

"You loved Lily for a very long time." He started to protest, but she held up a hand. "You hardly know me. I know you don't want to admit this, even to yourself, but I'm afraid you're enamored with me because of my fame. Please, I've seen this play out too many times. Don't do this to Lily or to me."

"I am enamored with you."

She nodded, as if she'd dialed in his motivation.

"But it has nothing to do with you being famous." He stepped in close and gently ran the tip of his finger over the top of her eyebrow and to the side of her eye. "I'm enamored with the sparkle in your deep-brown eyes and the way I can see into your soul, connect with you in a single glance. Like I did the first time I saw you."

Her eyes softened.

He reached for her hand and threaded their fingers together. "I'm enamored with the softness of your hands and the unique way they make me feel when you touch me and when I touch you. I've never felt an inspiring touch like yours, not in my lifetime."

Releasing her hand, he wove his fingers through her hair, massaging her scalp. "I'm enamored with your mind, the way you talk, our banter, the way you think, how smart and talented you are, your bravery, resiliency, and independence."

She blinked quickly, but her dark eyes were bright and beguiling.

He kept his hand in her hair and lifted his other one, slowly trailing the pad of his thumb over her soft lower lip. She moaned softly and her lips parted at his touch. All he wanted to do was kiss her, but he had to finish. "I'm enamored with your lips. The way you sass and tease me with them, your unique and barking laughter, and your kiss. I could never get enough of these lips."

He bent slowly down, giving her time to pull away or turn her head. She didn't. She arched up to him and their lips met. Instantly he was swept away in the connection and love and sparks that only existed for him with Eva.

When they pulled away for air, they were both breathing hard. He wanted to hold and kiss her until he had to go back to base in a few days. Did she feel the same?

Blinking quickly, she stepped back. His arms fell to the side and he felt empty, hollow. He needed her in his arms, but he would never force her there.

"I need time to think," she said. "To sort this out."

"What do you need to sort out?"

She peered up at him. "You loved Lily for thirteen years, yet you dropped her like a hot rock because you met me."

Miles was surprised at her vehemence. Especially after his words and that beautiful kiss. "Eva. Lily was a good friend, a wonderful person, but we should've broken up years ago."

"Why didn't you?"

"Time goes by quick, and the SEALs is a demanding career. I didn't talk to her much and saw her even less. For years, every time I went home and realized that things had fizzled, I'd ask her to date other people. She'd ask if I wanted to and I'd always say no. I was focused on my career, not dating. Six months ago, I was determined to end it. She broke down and sobbed and I felt awful. I didn't end it, and I had no idea that she was dealing with ... a hard situation, and having a military boyfriend protected her."

"Oh, no. Will she be okay?"

It was so like Eva to be more worried about Lily than her own pain. He did know her well, even if they'd had little time.

"I hope so. She promised to turn to Clint if she needed help or was in danger."

"Okay."

He waited, then continued, "I know the timing was off, breaking up with Lily after I met you. I'm sorry about that. I should've ended it long ago."

"But I gave you the motivation?" Her voice was still sharp.

"You could say that. What we have is unique and incredible, Eva. If you feel that like I do, please give me a chance. Let me date you, get to know you, be there for you. Please don't give up on us because our beginning was uncomfortable."

Eva pushed out a heavy breath. "I don't know, Miles."

His gut churned.

"Let me rest and ... we can talk later."

"Okay." He'd let her process and rest. He'd pray. Hard. "I'll bring takeout. Six? Thai, Mexican, sushi, Vietnamese?"

"Vietnamese," she said.

"Okay." He turned to the door. He had a strong aversion to leaving her. It couldn't be about her safety. Aiden's men were watching the security feed and monitoring her property, and the threats were gone.

He wanted to be in her presence, and he was afraid she was pushing him away for good.

No. This discomfort would go away. He'd come back and they'd eat and talk some more. She was overwrought. She needed time to process. She'd not only been attacked and had nefarious men after her, had to be uprooted from her home, but she'd fallen in love in a day and a half. Well, he hoped she'd fallen for him. The fact that he wasn't certain made his palms sweaty.

Glancing back over his shoulder as he stepped through the

door, he said, "Eva, I was loyal to Lily for thirteen years, no matter how many women hit on me or how my buddies or brothers teased me."

Her forehead wrinkled. "I don't want you giving up a thirteen-year relationship for me."

He shook his head. "I didn't. It was past time we broke it off, and Lily agreed. We were dating in name only. What I'm trying to do is brag a little. Which I don't usually do."

She studied him. "I know that about you, and I appreciate it."

"Thank you." He swallowed and continued, "I was loyal to Lily, and she lived hours away and our relationship was stagnant and forced. What you and I have is special and we hardly know each other. Those feelings are going to grow, deepen, and flourish, and I promise I will be fiercely loyal to you."

Her mouth opened and then she put her fingertips to her lips. He imagined she was remembering their intense kisses and wanted to give her more to strengthen his case. He stepped through the door and onto her small front porch instead. "Lock this and arm the system."

She shut it in his face. He heard the deadbolt turn and the beep of the alarm system. Good.

Miles smiled ruefully at her all but slamming the door in his face. He brushed his hand through his hair. He missed his cowboy hat.

Turning, he knew he should pull up an Uber, but he started walking instead. It was only a couple miles to Aiden's house. He needed to move and process and pray. Eva might finally trust that he would be loyal to her, and then again, she might slam the door in his face.

He had no idea which direction it would go tonight.

CHAPTER
Seventeen

EVA WATCHED Miles out of the peephole. Everything about him appealed to her, especially his humility, his bravery, his toughness, and his ability to see past her acting and into her heart. His magical touch, enchanting eyes, and all-consuming kiss swept her away.

But could she trust him? Would he really be fiercely loyal to her as their relationship grew and flourished? She loved the image and hope of that, but she'd had that hope before.

Yet Miles was right. What they had was incredible and special. He swore he'd never felt it before, and she knew she never had. She could understand holding onto a lackluster relationship for safety from Lily's side and not to hurt Lily in Miles's mind. He was that good of a guy, and she appreciated that he hadn't kissed her until he'd broken things off with Lily. She wanted to trust him and build a relationship together.

He walked away to the north, and she went to her bedroom

and forced herself to lie down. After half an hour of tossing and turning and daydreaming of Miles, she climbed out of bed, walked into her living room, and said into one of the cameras, "I'm going on a walk on the beach. You're welcome to follow me if you feel it's necessary."

"On my way," a male voice said through the camera.

She jumped and then barked out a surprised laugh. "I didn't know you could talk back."

"Yes, ma'am."

Laughing again, she waited for the knock on the door, then she and her guard Tyler headed across her patio and along the sand. It was a gorgeous late August afternoon. A lot warmer than Montana. She walked into the ocean and let her feet and legs get soaked with the cold sting of salt water.

When she got back to the house, she thanked Tyler and glanced at her watch. Five-thirty. Miles would be here soon. She wanted to talk to him, be with him, kiss him, but she was nervous about whether they could make it work. Would she take the plunge and try or would the deep-seated fear of more pain and the fact that Hollywood and military relationships were difficult ruin their chances?

Changing into a fitted T-shirt dress, she smiled to herself, thinking how Miles had liked her T-shirt nightgown that she'd had in Montana. She refreshed her makeup, sprayed on some coconut body splash, and paced the main room, tempted to say something to her buddies watching the camera.

A loud rap came on the back patio door, and she startled. Her heart leapt. Had Miles come up the beach from Aiden's house? She hurried over, peering through the glass, and her heart dropped. Not Miles.

Lake. Ah, shoot. She had to get rid of him. She didn't want him here when Miles showed up. Miles was humbly confident and wouldn't be threatened by Lake, but Lake would posture and be annoying.

"Miss Chevron?" the guard said through the camera walkie-talkie thingy.

"It's fine. It's Lake Eastwood."

"Oh." Obviously the guard knew who Lake was.

She turned off the alarm and yanked the door open. "Lake, get your hind quarters off of my property before I sic my guard dogs on you."

"Always so eloquent." Lake smiled rather than scowling like he had the past few times she'd seen him. "You look stunning, Eva. Are you doing all right? Did they catch the loser that was after you?"

"Yes." She nodded and leaned against the doorframe, folding her arms across her chest. "What's your damage, Lake?"

His handsome face lit up in a smile, but there was something lurking in his blue eyes. He was up to something, and it wouldn't bode well for her. Lake was so self-consumed he never thought about anyone but himself. She glanced around for paparazzi, but the beach appeared quiet.

"I was worried about you," he said smoothly. "Can we talk? It's beautiful out here." He gestured to the patio.

"For a minute," she said, rolling her eyes and walking out to the patio. It was better with Lake to let him talk, and then she might have a chance of getting him out of here before Miles arrived. She focused on the ocean and quiet stretch of beach rather than look at him. "What do you need?"

"You." She glanced at him and saw a flash of sun reflected off metal. He shoved a small pistol into her abdomen with his right hand, wrapping his left arm around her waist and yanking her close to his side. The cameras behind her would only see him cuddling her to his side.

"Lake!" she screamed, too stunned to feel terror. He had never shown any violent tendencies, only selfish ones.

"Don't," he warned. "I'll shoot. I couldn't care less at this point."

"Lake, are you nuts?" She looked around for her security guard. She'd just told the camera it was fine. Should she scream? Would Lake really shoot her?

"Let's walk, and don't you dare scream or act off or I will shoot." He shoved the gun harder.

Eva walked stiffly by his side as he directed her off the patio and into the sand, trying to edge away from the gun. Cold prickles stung her skin. He'd lost his mind.

"Lake, this isn't like you. What's going on? What do you need?"

"You ruined me," he snarled at her.

"How did I ruin you?"

They plunged through the sand and into the chilly water. Her guards would come. Right? Miles? Was it even time for him to be there? If Miles came, would Lake shoot her before Miles could reach them?

"I haven't gotten a role since you broke up with me," Lake said. "Everybody adores you, and it's all your fault that I've been blackballed."

"My fault? You cheated on *me*."

He angled her deeper into the water, his hand digging into her side as he held her close. She heard the high whine of a motor.

He shoved the gun harder into her ribs. She winced. "Jorge is going to pay me a load of money to bring you to him. I had no choice but to accept his offer since my acting career is washed up. I'm taking the cash and retiring on a beach somewhere."

"Jorge?"

"He's desperate for you and paying me much more than he would anyone else because I have the connection to get him out of prison."

The motor approached and suddenly a WaveRunner plowed through the surf and into the shallower water in front of them. A teenage boy was driving it.

"Turn it around," Lake demanded.

"Okay, sheesh." The kid flipped it around and held it as the waves lifted the machine up and down. He looked at Eva in awe. "You're Eva Chevron."

"Help," she begged.

"Shut up," Lake yelled at her. He looked at the young man. "I paid you a load. Now keep your mouth shut and take off running."

"Sorry, Eva." The kid jumped into the surf and dashed off to the north.

Lake shoved Eva onto the machine in front of him, climbing on behind her. She didn't know if he would shoot; she doubted Jorge would pay him for a dead Eva Chevron. She was dead either way if he got her out of here.

She heard shouts from behind her. Lake turned to look. She slugged him in the gut and threw herself to the right, trying to get off the machine.

"No!" Lake hollered. Her pinned her with his arms and gunned the WaveRunner into the ocean.

A large wave slapped the front, flinging the machine up and

threatening to spill them off. Lake busted through the wave and sped away from the beach.

Eva screamed in horror and dug her fingernails into his arm, trying to pry her way past the steel bands of his arms.

She'd rather be dead than in Jorge's or Lake's power.

CHAPTER
Eighteen

MILES WAITED IMPATIENTLY until finally it was five-forty and he could drive to the nearby Vietnamese place he'd found good reviews for on Google. The food was ready. He paid and was on his way to Eva's.

He pulled up front and hurried to her door, carrying the food. He rapped on the door and waited and waited. His gut churned. Was she going to ignore him? Was she even home? Had they made any progress, or was he dealing with more setbacks in her trusting him and his loyalty to her?

Loud footsteps pounded toward him from the street. Turning, he saw two of Aiden's guys running his direction.

"Lieutenant Miles," one of them shouted. "Lake Eastwood is rushing Eva away from her back patio."

Lake Eastwood? What? Why?

Miles didn't waste time asking questions. He dropped the food, rushed around the side of the house, vaulted over the fence, and ran to the back patio. One glance around confirmed she wasn't there. He hurried down the sand, looking around. The two guards were only a few steps behind him, guns drawn.

There! Lake was shoving Eva onto a WaveRunner. She was fighting him, but he gunned up and over a wave.

"Stop!" Miles roared.

"I don't dare shoot," he heard one of the guards yell. They were a moving target and with Eva trying to fight, she could easily get in the way of the shot.

"Get help," Miles hollered. "Coast Guard and police."

He kicked off his shoes, flung his shirt over his head, and hit the water at a run. He pushed through with high steps until he could dive under the first wave. Then he was in his element, swimming powerful strokes out through the ocean. But even he couldn't catch a WaveRunner gunning away from him.

He swam with every ounce of strength, determination, and skill he possessed. He could hear the WaveRunner moving farther away from him, out into the deeper ocean waves. Where was Lake taking her? Was her ex-boyfriend somehow involved in the last forty-eight hours and the hits on the dark web?

If they were meeting up with a boat, Eva's chances of survival or rescue were dwindling.

Miles had always believed he could triumph and protect. Eva was the most important protection detail he'd ever had, and he was failing her.

He swam harder, faster, but his arms were fatiguing. The WaveRunner was pulling farther away. No!

Please, Father above, please help Eva. I can't get to her. Please save her.

Despair filled him. Bitterness coated his throat. A wave broke over his head as he was turning for a breath. His mouth and lungs filled with salt water instead of oxygen. He sputtered. He'd never made a mistake like that in the ocean. Not normally.

Please. I need help. More importantly, Eva needs help.

Miles had been labeled a 'humble hero' many times, but he'd never been truly humble like this. He coughed and coughed. He didn't care if he drank the ocean. A Navy SEAL drowning was actually kind of comical.

He would be fine. The ocean wouldn't consume him. But Eva … she was in desperate danger. All he cared about was her safety.

The high whine of the motor disappeared. Miles popped to the surface, focusing on the Waverunner as he caught a breath and expelled salt water.

Nobody was on the machine. It was turning in a circle, a safety feature that happened when the rider fell off with the safety key attached to their wrist. He searched nearby and could see Eva's dark hair as she swam desperately his direction.

A boat was approaching from the south. It was pale blue, a brand-new cabin cruiser. Definitely not the Coast Guard's distinctive white with a red stripe down the bow.

"Miles," Eva cried out.

Lake's dark blond head was behind her. The sun framed them from the west, but Miles swore he could see fury in Lake's blue eyes.

"Eva!" Miles hollered, plowing through the water. He didn't feel fatigue. The water strengthened and buoyed him as he sliced through it toward Eva.

"Mi—" Eva's call was closer but ended in a garbled scream.

Miles looked up to see Lake shoving Eva under the water, his face distorted in an ugly glower.

"No!" Miles stroked through the water, praying Lake didn't drown Eva before he could reach them.

Lake saw him coming too late. Miles barreled into the man with his shoulder, knocking him away.

"Hey!"

Miles used his legs to propel his body up above the waves, rising above the water like a vengeful Poseidon, giving him the angle to slam his fist into Lake's nose. Blood spurted. The man cursed and finally released Eva. She popped up, her arms and legs churning as she gasped and sputtered and coughed.

The WaveRunner was close by, bobbing in the waves.

Miles grasped Eva around the waist, tugged her to the machine, and hefted her up. "Grab the handles."

She did, propelling herself up. "Miles!"

Lake lunged at him from behind, wrapping his elbow around his neck and choking him. The hold wasn't tight enough, allowing Miles enough slack to twist and slam his elbow back into the man's chin. Lake cursed but didn't let go.

The boat was bearing down on them. Miles could see a crew that definitely wasn't here to help him and Eva.

"Go," he gritted out to Eva, pointing toward the shore where her bodyguards would be waiting.

"No," she cried out, thankfully staying on the machine as she continued to cough out the water from her near-drowning.

She wouldn't leave without him. Shoot. She needed to. Miles could duck under the water and swim back to shore before the boat knew where he'd disappeared to, but Eva's safety was all that mattered.

He ducked down into the water, taking Lake with him. The man's grip slackened, and Miles shoved his arms off. He pivoted and rotated Lake around in front of him, then grabbed Lake's arm. As he surfaced, he kept Lake's face underwater and yanked on his arm until he heard a pop.

Lake's garbled scream assured him the man's shoulder had come clear of the socket. With a dislocated shoulder, he wouldn't be choking Miles anytime soon, drowning Eva, or following them.

"Miles," Eva cried out, reaching for him.

"Scoot up on the machine," he urged.

Lake surfaced, whining and cursing them.

The pale blue boat was a hundred feet away, slowing to approach them.

Miles dodged behind the WaveRunner, grabbed the sides, and pulled himself up. It rocked dangerously. If they went in, they'd be in trouble.

He heard more motors approaching from the northeast. That didn't make sense. He glanced over and saw two WaveRunners angling their direction from the beach. Miles had no idea whose side they were on. He couldn't make out their faces yet.

"Mr. Eastwood?" a man called from the boat.

"Shoot them!" Lake screamed. "Kill them!"

Miles pressed the button to start the WaveRunner. They needed distance and they needed it now.

The machine didn't start.

Lake held up the bracelet with the key that disengaged the motor when the rider fell off, grinning viciously as the blood from his nose mixed with the water.

"Kill them!" he screamed.

Men appeared at the railing of the boat, aiming assault rifles down at them. Miles grabbed Eva and yanked her off the machine, falling to the side that would give them some cover and concealment.

Shots rang out. He tugged Eva under the water, praying she'd be okay after almost drowning half a minute ago. Her eyes were wide and terrified.

He wrapped one arm around her waist and angled them in the water away from the boat. He feared they wouldn't get enough distance before Eva needed to surface. Unfortunately, it wasn't dark enough outside to hide.

The WaveRunners from shore were suddenly in his vision.

Eva tugged at his arm. He had to let her surface and get some oxygen. He cradled her in his arms to shield her. If anybody was getting shot, it was him. He eased them up out of the water and encouraged, "Take a breath quick."

She gasped for air.

He heard more shots and instinctively safeguarded her. Men were yelling. The boat motor roared to life. He hoped Eva had gotten enough air as he prepared to take her under and attempt an escape. He needed the Coast Guard to show up. Soon.

"Lieutenant Coleville," a man yelled.

He looked toward the voice and blinked in surprise. Aiden's guards. Josh and Tyler. On WaveRunners, taking shots at the retreating boat.

Kicking to keep himself and Eva up, a wave slapped him in the face. He didn't care. He spit and stared.

The pale blue boat was speeding away to the south.

"You all right?" Josh called. "Eva?"

"We're both okay." Miles looked down at her. She coughed and looked half-drowned, but she was breathing and she was in his arms. "Are you okay?"

She nodded, clinging to his wet shirt. "Miles. Oh, thank you."

The whine of a WaveRunner surprised him. He looked up to

see Lake pressing on the accelerator awkwardly with his left hand, his right arm hanging uselessly.

A shot rang out. Lake screeched as blood spurted from his left hand. He fell off the WaveRunner again.

Miles whipped around to see Tyler grinning.

"Nice shot," he said.

Josh eased his WaveRunner over and Miles helped lift Eva out of the water and up behind the security guard.

Another boat raced in their direction. Miles tensed, squinting. White with a red stripe. *Oh, please.*

"U.S. Coast Guard," came through a bullhorn.

"Finally," Tyler muttered, coming over toward Miles with his WaveRunner.

Miles climbed on. He'd never been so relieved to be out of the water. He looked over at Eva, who was leaning her head against Josh's back, still pulling in deep breaths of air, her hair hanging around her face. Her dark eyes focused on him, and she smiled.

Miles could hear Lake not far away, still cursing and now moaning in pain. The Coast Guard would take some time to sort this out, and he was afraid Lake's associates in the boat were long gone. But Eva was safe.

Thank you, he breathed. His prayers had been answered.

CHAPTER
Nineteen

EVA WAS DRAINED. Completely. They'd finally gotten through the Coast Guard questioning, then the police questioning, then the FBI had come in with more questioning. Through it all, Miles had stayed by her side. Aiden had shown up halfway through the FBI questioning. That made everything go a lot smoother. Their respect for Captain Aiden Porter bordered on worship.

She and Miles were at Aiden's house. She took a long shower in one of the guest bedrooms downstairs, reveling in knowing that Miles was in the next bedroom over.

Dressing in a comfortable T-shirt and shorts that Aiden had given her, she brushed out her hair, put on some lotion, and walked into the bedroom. She only wanted Miles. Opening the door to the hallway, intent on finding him, she saw Miles leaning against the opposite wall.

Miles. Her military cowboy. He would always be there for her. He was so loyal he'd swam through the ocean like Poseidon and risked his life covering her with his body when the bullets flew. This man would never leave her for a more famous option. Her Miles was one hundred percent devoted to her, and she believed he always would be.

His blue eyes lit up as he saw her. He pushed away from the wall and hurried toward her.

"Eva." He gently wrapped his hands around her waist, framing it with his large palms, his thumbs brushing her abdomen.

"Miles." She collapsed against him, wrapping her arms around his back and drawing strength from him. "Oh, Miles, thank you. You were like Poseidon in the water. You saved me. It was miraculous."

He cradled her close, sliding his hands around to her lower back and kissing her forehead. "I prayed so hard. I think God saved you and you saved yourself fighting free of Lake and getting off the WaveRunner. You are so brave, Eva."

They'd rehashed the story time and again with the authorities, but she could still feel the miraculous power of heaven. She hadn't thought she'd ever fight free of Lake's grip, but she had, and then Miles had somehow appeared in the ocean like a merman or, more accurately, a highly-trained Navy SEAL.

Josh and Tyler had sprinted down the beach and been able to commandeer some WaveRunners from the pier over a mile away. Neither of them could swim like Miles and hadn't dared attempt it. She didn't know anybody that could swim like Miles. He was definitely her hero.

"You saved me. Thank you." She arched up and kissed him.

Miles met her halfway, and she was swept away with the desire and joy from his kiss. Miles surrounded her with his strength and lifted her with his kiss, protecting her and making her believe in a future with him.

"Oh!" Aiden's voice interrupted their kiss as he appeared at the bottom of the stairs. "Forgive me, friends, but somebody said Vietnamese food, and I missed dinner in my rush to fly to you. Are you joining us? Tyler and Josh want to brag about Miles being Aquaman one more time."

Eva stared up into Miles's blue eyes. "Miles isn't Aquaman. Too pure. Though I admit he moves like Aquaman in the water."

Miles smiled. "I need a few dozen more tattoos to be Aquaman."

"Let's stick with Poseidon then," Eva said.

Aiden chuckled. "Dinner?"

"I'm not hungry," Eva said, hoping Miles wasn't either.

"I am," Miles said, mischief filling his blue eyes.

"Oh. Okay. We can eat." They would have plenty of time to talk and kiss later. She hoped. She eased back.

Miles tugged her in tight again. "I'm hungry for your lips."

Aiden chuckled again as Eva's heart raced.

"That was cheesy," Aiden said. "I'll leave you two alone. We'll save you some."

"Thank you," Miles said, his head already descending toward hers.

"Yes, thank you," Eva echoed. "For everything."

"Think nothing of it." There was laughter in Aiden's voice. His footsteps retreated.

Miles stopped a breath away from Eva's lips. "Before I devour these luscious lips." He winked. "Does this mean you trust I'll be loyal to you until the day I die, and you're willing to give us a shot?"

Eva studied him. She loved him, though it was far too early

to tell him that. "You're my hero, Lieutenant Miles Coleville. You protected me from being shot. The least I can do is let you woo me, date me, impress me, and devour me with your lips."

Miles chuckled and kissed her, but it was much softer and shorter than their previous kisses. "Eva," he whispered roughly against her lips. "I do want to devour your lips, but I need you to know … you're my match, the woman I want to spend every spare minute with. You're special and unique to me. Our connection and sparks are unparalleled. I feel heaven above brought us together. I hope you're ready for the most fiercely loyal Navy SEAL cowboy to be completely devoted to you and spend every moment I'm not on a mission waiting on your doorstep or on the set to your latest movie. Wherever you are, that's where I want to be."

Eva's spirit soared with his words. "I shouldn't admit this. It's far too soon. But I love you, Miles. When I saw you running on the beach, haloed with the sun, I had been praying for the good Lord to send me a man I could trust. He did. I hope *you're* ready for the most fiercely loyal hick actress to be completely devoted to you."

He grinned and then he captured her mouth with his. She was swept away in the passion and love he felt for her. She didn't have to choose to trust or love Miles. She felt both so deeply, she knew they would be devoted to each other. For this life and beyond.

His kiss was magic, their connection unparalleled. She could hardly wait to prove her own loyalty to him and grow closer each day.

Thank you for reading Miles and Eva's story! Keep reading for an unedited excerpt of Lieutenant Paul Braven and Shay Cannon's romance, The Pilot & The Athlete.

I know you're all wondering about Lily Lillywhite and the danger she's in. Her story is coming soon, paired with the closed-off Sheriff Clint Coleville in a marriage for protection detail - *The Sheriff & the Nurse.*

Hugs and thanks for all the support and love,
Cami

Coleville Ranch Romance

The Recluse & The Fugitive – Cade Miller and Jacqueline Oliver

The Bodyguard & The Billionaire – Lieutenant Hays West and Elizabeth Oliver

The Soldier & The Actress - Lieutenant Miles Coleville and Eva Chevron

The Pilot & The Athlete – Lieutenant Paul Braven and Shay Cannon

The Sheriff & the Nurse – Clint Coleville and Lily Lillywhite

The Roper & The Author – Walker Coleville and Marci Richards

The Female Warrior and The Charming Gentleman – Jarom Love and Autumn Cardon

A Chance for Charity

Impossible Treasure - Captain Cash Trapper and Brylee Auburn

Impossible Escape - Major Bennett Mason and Rose Lillywhite

Impossible Sail - Captain Eli Grant and Livvy Benedict

Impossible Climb – Lieutenant Quaid Raven (Thomas Oliver) and Anna Marley

Impossible Crusade - Captain Aiden Porter and Chalisa Anderson

Impossible Thrills - Lieutenant Nick Jacobs and Darcy Saint

Impossible Chase – Captain Jagger Lemuel and Belinda Ralphs

Impossible Rapids - Shawn Hollister and Julie Pandoran

The Pilot & The Athlete

Jonah yanked her out of Lyle's arms. He shoved her toward the closest chair, pushed her down, and grabbed her seatbelt. Clicking it in place, his fingers lingered on her abdomen. He leaned in close and she wished she could vomit again.

She ducked her head. He grabbed her chin and forced her face up toward his. She pushed out a breath of air that she hoped smelled as horrid as her mouth tasted. His leering expression changed to disgust.

"You stink," he snarled. "Lyle, give me a water bottle and some gum or a breath mint or something."

The man hurried to the rear of the plane then back to them, handing over a water bottle and a box of breath mints.

Jonah opened the water bottle and poured some in her mouth. She swished it around and spit it in his face.

"Hey!" Jonah raised his hand to smack her. She wanted to cower but she glowered at him instead. If she was going to die, she was going to die as an American Olympian, proud and brave, not cowering to a scum like this.

His eyes narrowed. Instead of hitting her, he grabbed her jaw and cheeks and squeezed so hard her mouth involuntarily popped open. He dumped a dozen strong mints in her mouth. She gagged and prayed she wouldn't choke. He sneered at her and forced her mouth to open and close, chewing up the mints.

Her breath no longer stunk. Her throat was now on fire and her minty taste was so powerful it might keep him away. For a minute.

"Buckle up, please," Paul's voice came across the plane's speakers.

It was Paul's voice. It *was* Paul. How could it be Paul and he not help her?

The other men obeyed, but Jonah didn't. He stayed leaning over her, smiling. His teeth were white but the front one was chipped. His breath smelled worse than hers had tasted.

The motor of the plane revved and she knew her life was over. They'd taxi out of here, lift into the air, and then the vile Jonah would 'have his fun' as Paul had said. She still couldn't wrap her mind around Paul Braven saying that or dismissing her. Tears stung at her eyes, disappointment in Paul not being a hero, pain of Jonah's harsh treatment, and fear of what was coming.

She blinked and glared at Jonah. She was going to fight and scratch and kick and bite and vomit and anything else she could think of. If she could, she'd force them to knock her out or kill her.

How had her life gotten to this low point?

The cockpit door flew open and banged loudly against the wall. Paul stood framed in it, a pistol in hand. His dark eyes filled with determination and confidence. He fired and shot in quick succession.

Lyle banged back against a seat, blood streaming from his forehead. Handsome Jaden sprawled to the side, blood streaming from his throat. Ross stood and yanked out his own pistol. Paul shot him square in the chest. He clutched at his chest and sunk into a seat. Paul fired again and he didn't move, his gun clattering to the floor.

Jonah sprawled over top of her and yelled, "You shoot me, she could die."

Paul did some tough guy from a movie type of drip move where he separated the two pieces of the gun and dropped them in different directions.

"I won't shoot you," he said, calm and heroic and perfect.

He was good and true and he was saving her. Shay's heart leapt with joy, though the foul and massive Jonah pressed on top of her was far from encouraging. Why had Paul dropped his gun?

Jonah arched back to look at Paul better, maybe surprised by the move too.

"I need someone for the police to question," Paul said with a smirk.

He dove across the space and slammed his fist into Jonah's cheek. He ripped the man off of her and shoved him back into another set of seats.

Jonah fought back, his fists a whirl as he hit at Paul.

She winced and cried out as Paul was driven back.

"No!"

Paul glanced at her and gave her a reassuring and beautiful smile. His white teeth, the skin crinkling at the edges of his eyes and mouth and slight dimples appearing in his cheeks made her heart race out of control for a completely different reason than it had all night.

Jonah roared and knocked Paul back with vicious hits.

Shay tried to jump up and help somehow. Her seatbelt held her fast. She fumbled to release it, but her hands were trembling too violently.

"Please help Paul win," she begged heaven above.

Paul gave her a smirk and said, "Ah come on Shay, a little faith. I was just making him feel like he had a chance."

Shay's eyes widened in surprise. Jonah cursed at him and swung even more viciously. Paul dodged Jonah's assault and moved in closer, which terrified Shay. Shouldn't they be running from this brute? Paul was strong, but he was tall and lean. Jonah was thick and would most likely fight dirty.

Paul drove the monster back into a chair with precise jabs. The muscles in Paul's back were outlined by the shirt and the striations in his arms were a work of art as he pummeled the now whining Jonah. He bloodied Jonah's nose and split his lip and Shay couldn't help but cheer. She didn't love violence but her hometown hero dismantling the man who would've raped and killed her was something to cheer for.

"Yay!" Shay cheered. "You're fire!"

Paul grinned and she knew all was right in the world.

Then a flash of metal appeared in Jonah's hand.

"Paul!" she shrieked.

Jonah would impale him and Paul would die trying to defend her.

Paul's hand darted out and grabbed Jonah's wrist. Jonah shrieked and she could swear she heard bones break. Jonah released the knife, grabbing his injured wrist and cursing.

"I'm done with you," Paul said, darting behind Jonah and

grasping his neck. The man flailed and then slumped into the chair.

Paul released him and straightened. His gaze swung to Shay. "One moment," he said with a warm smile. The words were a promise. In one moment Paul would come for her and she would hug him tight.

He darted back into the cockpit and returned moments later with a backpack. Swooping his gun off the ground, he put the pieces together and the gun in a holster on his hip. He tugged open the backpack, pulled out a length of rope and hurried to shove the unconscious Jonah onto his face on the floor and tie him up with his legs and hands bound together. She was stunned and awed by him. Gratitude filled her. It was a marvel how quick she'd gone from imminent death to inspiring rescue.

Paul glanced at the other men as if confirming they were dead. Shay's gut churned again. Paul had killed three men to save her life. She would be forever grateful, but the loss of more life sickened her and she prayed it wouldn't be disturbing to Paul.

He turned to her and the oxygen rushed out of her lungs. He was the epitome of every girlish dream she'd ever had. He was disheveled from the fight with Jonah, and it only made him more appealing. He'd fought and won. Rescued her from death and from worse things than death. He'd come for her.

She let out a whimper and sprung up to hug him fiercely. Well, she tried. Her seat belt caught her and she got nowhere.

Paul's brown eyes filled with concern. He hurried to her and bent down, easily unclasping the seat belt. The soft brush of his fingers against her abdomen and the appealing warmth that rose from his fingers were such a contrast to the other men's touches that more tears came to her eyes.

"Shay," his voice was gentle. "You're okay now. It's over. I'm here."

"You saved me!" she cried out. She flung her arms around his neck and she kissed him.

Paul startled and she feared she'd been too impetuous.

Then he returned the kiss. He pressed her back into the seat and he took command of her lips with warm, persuasive, delicious movements of his lips that changed her entire vision of this night.

She was not only safe, warm, and cherished, she was full of sparks, light, and had found the love of her life. He tasted clean and fresh. He smelled like sandalwood and musk. The most perfect manly smell on earth.

Paul broke away from the kiss, straightened, and helped her to her feet. She was stunned and disoriented.

"We've got to go," he said, his voice urgent. He slung his backpack over his shoulder.

"You'll never escape," Jonah snarled at them, peering up at them from the floor.

Shay startled. She hadn't realized he woke up.

"Watch us," Paul shot back.

Keep reading *The Pilot & The Athlete* on Amazon.

Also by Cami Checketts

Coleville Ranch Romance

The Recluse & The Fugitive – Cade Miller and Jacqueline Oliver

The Bodyguard & The Billionaire – Lieutenant Hays West and Elizabeth Oliver

The Soldier & The Actress - Lieutenant Miles Coleville and Eva Chevron

The Pilot & The Athlete – Lieutenant Paul Braven and Shay Cannon

The Sheriff & the Nurse – Clint Coleville and Lily Lillywhite

The Roper & The Author – Walker Coleville and Marci Richards

The Female Warrior and The Charming Gentleman – Jarom Love and Autumn Cardon

A Chance for Charity

Impossible Treasure - Captain Cash Trapper and Brylee Auburn

Impossible Escape - Major Bennett Mason and Rose Lillywhite

Impossible Sail - Captain Eli Grant and Livvy Benedict

Impossible Climb – Lieutenant Quaid Raven (Thomas Oliver) and Anna Marley

Impossible Crusade - Captain Aiden Porter and Chalisa Anderson

Impossible Thrills - Lieutenant Nick Jacobs and Darcy Saint

Impossible Chase – Captain Jagger Lemuel and Belinda Ralphs

Impossible Rapids - Shawn Hollister and Julie Pandoran

Billionaire Bodyguard Romance

Protecting the Athlete - Lieutenant Ike Porter and Myra Tueller

Christmas in Augustine

The Royal Captain and the Designer – Captain Levi Favor and Faith Radisson

The Wounded Guard and the Royal Stylist – Lieutenant Brad Rivera and Arianna Gunnell

The Impulsive Princess and the Soldier – Captain Mason Henson and Princess Kiera August

Sweet Royal Romance Suspense

The General Prince and the Nerd – General Prince Raymond August and Macey Summers

The Brave Prince and the Teacher – Prince Curtis August and Aliya Drummond

The Doctor Prince and the Outsider – Doctor Prince Steffan August and Hattie Ballard

The Ninja Prince and the Investigator – Prince Derek August and Ellery Monson

The Charming Prince and the Single Mum – Prince Malik August and Sophie Pederson

The Crown Prince and the Traitor – Prince Tristan August and Jennifer Shule

The Police Chief and the Musician – Chief Jensen Allendale and Livvy Moser

The Royal Major and the Executive – Chad Major Prescott and Hope Radisson

The Grieving King and the Emissary – King Nolan August and Madeline Prescott

Billionaire Protection Romances

Matchmaking the Singer and the Warrior – Gray Denizen (Smokey G) and Sara Sanderson

Matchmaking the Duchess and the Commander – Commander Blaine Lewis and Duchess Catherine Baldwin Lewis

Matchmaking the Entertainer and the Firefighter – Magnum Porter Israelsen and Ariel Chadwick

Matchmaking the Model and the Beast – Hayden "Beast" Warren and Eva Canterbury

Matchmaking the Spy and the Heiress – Gage Remington and Cassandra Mickelson

Matchmaking the Bodyguard and the Philanthropist – Petty Officer Manuel Leandro "Wolf" and Sadie Ballard

Summit Valley Christmas Romance

His Perfect Match for Christmas – Captain "Cap" Zeke Hendrickson and Mia Burton

His Ski Resort Overrun for Christmas – Jace Jardine and Ayla Thurston

His Cabin Invaded for Christmas – Ammon Jardine and Ivy Collier

His Unexpected Wedding for Christmas – Lieutenant Van Udy "Chaos" and Melodee Granger

Delta Family Romances

Deceived – Colton Delta and Bailey Ashworth

Abandoned – Thor Delta and Shelley Vance

Committed – Klein Vance and Alivia Delta

Betrayed – Greer Delta and Emery Reeder

Devoted – Esther Delta and Sheriff Reed Peterson

Compromised – Lieutenant Aiden Delta and Melene Collier

Endangered – Chandler Delta and Kylee Seamons

Accepted – Lieutenant Braden Moyle and Maddie Delta

Returned – Hudson Delta and Kelsey James

Devastated – Jessie Delta and Chief Petty Officer Zander "Demo" Povey

Famous Friends Romances

Loving the Firefighter

Loving the Athlete

Loving the Rancher

Loving the Coach

Loving the Contractor

Loving the Sheriff

Loving the Entertainer

The Hidden Kingdom Romances

Royal Secrets – Prince Bodi Magnum and Julia Adams

Royal Security – Princess Adelaide (Addie) Magnum and Malik Sherwood

Royal Doctor – Commander Alaric and Doctor Grace Johannson

Royal Mistake – Princess Belle Magnum and Stuart Falslev

Royal Courage – Princess Leia Magnum and Wes Hunsaker

Royal Pilot – Treck Wilder and Haven Ahlstrom

Royal Imposter – Crown Prince Quinn Magnum and Stella Watkins

Royal Baby – General Kingston Magnum and Reagan Anderson

Royal Battle – Princess Constance Magnum and Samson Cohen

Royal Fake Fiancé – Prince Darian Magnum and Zara Nelson

Secret Valley Romance

Sister Pact

Marriage Pact

Christmas Pact

Survive the Romance

Romancing the Treasure

Romancing the Escape

Romancing the Boat

Romancing the Mountain

Romancing the Castle

Romancing the Extreme Adventure

Romancing the Island

Romancing the River

Romancing the Spartan Race

Mystical Lake Resort Romance

Only Her Undercover Spy

Only Her Cowboy

Only Her Best Friend

Only Her Blue-Collar Billionaire

Only Her Injured Stuntman

Only Her Amnesiac Fake Fiancé

Only Her Hockey Legend

Only Her Smokejumper Firefighter

Only Her Christmas Miracle

Jewel Family Romance

Do Marry Your Billionaire Boss – Joshua Jewel and Jace Jardine

Do Trust Your Special Ops Bodyguard – Isaac Jewel and Cosette Peterson

Do Date Your Handsome Rival – Luke Jewel and Marietta Valez

Do Rely on Your Protector – Seth Jewel and Breeze Cain

Do Kiss the Superstar – Caleb Jewel and Emily Gehring

Do Tease the Charming Billionaire – Rachel Jewel and Abe Bradford

Do Claim the Tempting Athlete – Eve Jewel and Beckett Tanner

Do Depend on Your Keeper – Allison Bradford and Birch Merrill

Strong Family Romance

Don't Date Your Brother's Best Friend

Her Loyal Protector

Don't Fall for a Fugitive

Her Hockey Superstar Fake Fiance

Don't Ditch a Detective

Don't Miss the Moment

Don't Love an Army Ranger

Don't Chase a Player

Don't Abandon the Superstar

Steele Family Romance

Her Dream Date Boss

The Stranded Patriot

The Committed Warrior

Extreme Devotion

Quinn Romance Adventures

Devoted & Deserted – Ryder Quinn and Bree Stevens

Conflicted & Famous – Caleb Quinn and Jasmine Peters

Gentle & Broken – Mack Quinn and Sariah Udy

Rugged & At-Risk – Griff Quinn and Scarlett Lily

Too-Perfect & Stranded – Navy Quinn and Holden Jennings

Rejected & Hidden – Colt Quinn and Kim Heathrow

Running Romcom

Running for Love

Taken from Love

Saved by Love

Cami's Collections

Billionaire Protection Romances Collection

Summit Valley Christmas Collection

Delta Family Romance Collection

Famous Friends Romance Collection

Secret Valley Romance Collection

Hidden Kingdom Romance Collection

Survive the Romance Collection

Mystical Lake Resort Romance Collection

Billionaire Boss Romance Collection

Jewel Family Collection

The Romance Escape Collection

Cami's Firefighter Collection

Strong Family Romance Collection

Steele Family Collection

Hawk Brothers Collection

Quinn Family Collection

Cami's Georgia Patriots Collection

Cami's Military Collection

Billionaire Beach Romance Collection

Billionaire Bride Pact Collection

Echo Ridge Romance Collection

Texas Titans Romance Collection

Snow Valley Collection

Christmas Romance Collection

Holiday Romance Collection

Extreme Sports Romance Collection

Georgia Patriots Romance

The Loyal Patriot

The Gentle Patriot

The Stranded Patriot

The Pursued Patriot

Jepson Brothers Romance

How to Design Love

How to Switch a Groom

How to Lose a Fiance

Billionaire Boss Romance

Her Dream Date Boss

Her Prince Charming Boss

Hawk Brothers Romance

The Determined Groom

The Stealth Warrior

Her Billionaire Boss Fake Fiance

Risking it All

Navy Seal Romance

The Protective Warrior

The Captivating Warrior

The Stealth Warrior

Texas Titan Romance

The Fearless Groom

The Trustworthy Groom

The Beastly Groom

The Irresistible Groom

The Determined Groom

Billionaire Beach Romance

Caribbean Rescue

Cozumel Escape

Cancun Getaway

Trusting the Billionaire

How to Kiss a Billionaire

Onboard for Love

Shadows in the Curtain

Billionaire Bride Pact Romance

The Resilient One

The Feisty One

The Independent One

The Protective One

The Faithful One

The Daring One

The Sassy One

Park City Firefighter Romance

Rescued by Love

Reluctant Rescue

Stone Cold Sparks

Snowed-In for Christmas

Echo Ridge Romance

Christmas Makeover

Last of the Gentlemen

My Best Man's Wedding

Change of Plans

Counterfeit Date

Snow Valley

Full Court Devotion: Christmas in Snow Valley

A Touch of Love: Summer in Snow Valley

Running from the Cowboy: Spring in Snow Valley

Light in Your Eyes: Winter in Snow Valley

Romancing the Singer: Return to Snow Valley

Fighting for Love: Return to Snow Valley

Other Books by Cami

Seeking Mr. Debonair: Jane Austen Pact

Seeking Mr. Dependable: Jane Austen Pact

Saving Sycamore Bay

Oh, Come On, Be Faithful

Protect This

Blog This

Redeem This

The Broken Path

Dead Running

Dying to Run

Fourth of July

Love & Loss

Love & Lies

The Recluse & The Fugitive

Cade Miller forked the mix of hay, grain, and the vitamins the vet had suggested to the sick herd still in the corral past the barn. With summer finally here, the rest of his cattle could graze in the pasture east of the lake.

Everything was quiet today. Even the birds seemed to be chirping less. Why?

Was something bad coming? His mom had called him her 'happy horse boy' as a child. He smiled at the memory, wondering what she called him now. Probably her 'ultra-tough military hero son'. His mom was proud of him and adored him. Nobody could claim he was happy.

His horses, cows, land, and solitude were all he needed. At least that was what he told his family and any persistent friends like Easton and Walker Coleville when they insisted on coming to visit, bringing him some of Millie's bread or cookies, wanting to get him out rock climbing, mountain biking, or doing tricks off the thirty-foot rock shelf into his lake. Those two never gave up. He appreciated their friendship and would never tell them that. Their brother Rhett had built his house, and they had a good relationship, but their brother Clint had ruined his life.

An eerie female scream came from up the south mountainside.

A cougar?

Cade dropped the pitchfork, slid his sidearm out of the holster, and hurried around the corral. The mountain lions usually left him alone, but they loved to tear his calves apart. It never hurt to be prepared if a predator was coming after his cattle.

A scream sounded again, and then he heard gravel dislodging as something slid down the mountainside. Or someone.

He was a couple hundred yards away, but he could see a pink T-shirt, dark hair, and a distinctively feminine body tumbling down the mountainside. The woman somersaulted headfirst into a tree branch, and her screaming stopped. Her body slowed its descent as the ground began to level out.

Cade stowed his 1911 and jumped into his Ranger. The side by side was a lot faster than he could run, and he might have to haul her to his truck and the hospital. Unless she was in bad enough shape that he'd need to call for a helicopter.

His pulse sped as he raced across the dirt path around the lake and toward the switchback trail. He rarely saw hikers or even mountain bikers this deep in the mountains.

She was lying about ten feet away from the southeast side of the lake. Her head was down, long dark hair spilling around it.

Cade jammed the vehicle into park, turned the key off, and

jumped out. Dropping to his knees next to her, he lifted some hair away and felt for a pulse. It was there and strong. That was good news.

Her head rolled to the side, and she groaned. So she had to be breathing. A goose egg was already forming on her forehead, but he didn't see any blood. Good. She was wearing a tight, long-sleeved pink shirt and black running pants. The material was ripped in multiple spots, scrapes and traces of blood, but no visibly broken bones.

He pulled out his phone to call for help when she rolled over to her back and blinked her eyes open.

Blue. Blue as his mountain lake or the Montana sky. Long-lashed eyes with shapely dark eyebrows and a sprinkling of freckles across her nose and sun-browned cheeks. Her lips were straight and wide—Julia Roberts type lips. He liked them.

He blinked and focused. She looked oddly familiar. Why?

"Ma'am? I'm going to call for help. Can you tell me what and where and how bad it hurts?" He was no kind of doctor, but his eight years in the military had taught him the basics. Living up here alone, he'd learned how to bind up his cattle or keep a horse alive until the vet arrived. But this was no cow or horse. This was a beautiful woman. How had she fallen down his mountainside?

She blinked at him as if not comprehending what he said, but then suddenly her eyes widened, and terror filled them.

"It's okay. You're safe," he said. Then something compelled him to add, "I won't let anybody come at you."

"No," she moaned, shaking her head. "She's coming."

"There now. We'll just call for help, and I'll keep you safe until the sheriff gets here." The sheriff. He loathed the sheriff and doubted Clint would come. He'd send a deputy to collect this beauty and avoid the confrontation with Cade.

"You cannot call." Those blue eyes were frantic. "No. She will come for me and torture or murder you."

She snatched the phone from his hand and hurled it away.

"What the …" Cade jumped to his feet to go retrieve his phone. What kind of woman threw someone's phone? She was obviously not herself. He hoped.

The phone plunked into the nearby lake. Not near the shoreline, either.

He stopped in his tracks and pivoted back, looking down at her. "Good arm," he muttered.

She smiled briefly, then jumped to her feet and rushed at him.

Cade eased back, holding up his hands. "Hey, hey."

He didn't get any more out. She grabbed his shirt and pulled herself closer. She was a decent height, maybe five-seven, and easily the most beautiful woman he'd ever seen. She put even his lost love Sheryl Dracon, who'd had the face of an angel, to shame. That was a huge compliment in his mind to this intense and probably unstable woman.

"She's coming," she said, her eyes gaining a wild edge. "She's coming. We have to hide, or she'll hurt you."

"Look, ma'am." He took her hands in his to pull them from his shirt, but the moment he wrapped his palms around her smaller hands, the ground shifted, he lost his train of thought, and warmth radiated up his arms and into his blood vessels, charging him with a heady mixture of yearning and purpose.

The blue-eyed beauty stared at him, then down at his hands around hers, then back up at him. She wobbled on her feet.

From the head injury or the ground-shaking he was experiencing?

Find *The Recluse & The Fugitive* on Amazon.

About the Author

Cami is a part-time author, part-time exercise consultant, part-time housekeeper, full-time wife, and overtime mother of four adorable boys. Sleep and relaxation are fond memories. She's never been happier.

Join Cami's VIP list to find out about special deals, giveaways and new releases and receive a free copy of *Seeking Mr. Debonair: The Jane Austen Pact* by clicking here.

cami@camichecketts.com
www.camichecketts.com

facebook.com/CamiCheckettsAuthor
x.com/camichecketts
instagram.com/camicheckettsbooks
bookbub.com/profile/cami-checketts
youtube.com/@camicheckettsbooks
tiktok.com/@camichecketts
amazon.com/stores/Cami-Checketts/author/B002NGXNC6